The first time it was the
This time the dan

SECOND
RESCUE

Kenneth Field

a sycamore tree book
from
Pacific Press® Publishing Association
Nampa, Idaho
Oshawa, Ontario, Canada

Edited by Jerry D. Thomas
Designed by Dennis Ferree
Cover art Alex Williams / Masterfile

Copyright © 1999 by
Pacific Press® Publishing Association
Printed in the United States of America
All Rights Reserved

Field, Kenneth Eugene.
    Second rescue: the first time it was the sea that nearly claimed
their lives. This time the danger could claim their souls / Kenneth Field.
        p.   cm.
    ISBN 0-8163-1690-2
    I. Title.
PS3556.I387S43   1999
813'.54—dc21   98-31515
                                                                    CIP

99 00 01 02 03 • 5 4 3 2 1

DEDICATION

for Carol, my wife, who always tells me the truth,
which I value beyond price . . .

for Janell, my friend, who once asked me if I was through
wandering my forty years in the wilderness . . .

for the Class of 1972—my brothers and sisters—
that we may never forget . . .

for Dr. Glade Birch, my tribal elder,
who reminded me where I came from . . .

for the men of W.I.N.,
who helped me find the dream and gave me hope.

CONTENTS

FOREWORD

Having faith—believing in something that occurred in the past as a guide for conducting our lives in the present—is all well and good. Believing that God created the world, that Moses led the Israelites out of Egypt, that Jesus died on the Cross for our sins, changes how we view what has gone before, and that is critical. But we must also believe that natural and supernatural forces are at work even now and will continue to work in the days ahead. Otherwise, we must concede that God has gone to sleep, at least so far as our present time is concerned. This means that there must be stories of faith, power, and grace in our day, too, . . . until, at last, we can go home.

*It began with light in the darkness . . . and a man
going nowhere special . . . and a dream
that changed everything.*

1

FLOTSAM

J. T. woke to the bedside clock radio singing to itself, the haunting voice of some young pop star musing over his loss of faith. His wife, Karen, would have pointed out that the "young" singer was actually his age, but he didn't voice his thoughts, and she was still asleep anyway. The song, however, seemed appropriate enough.

Swinging his feet out of bed, J. T. lurched to his feet and stumbled down the hall to the bathroom, running his left hand along the wall for guidance and balance. He blinked at the wash of light above the bathroom sink and wondered why it didn't seem quite as bright as he remembered it.

"Light," he muttered. "Something about light."

The family dog nudged him then danced backward with a grin on her pushed-in face when he glanced down at her. He knew what she wanted, of course. And she knew that he knew. A person only had to look her in the eyes to see that. If he said the magic word, she'd scuttle around the living room in a doggy frenzy that ended at the front door.

So he said it.

"Walk?"

And she did it.

A morning ritual of sorts . . . one way to begin the day. He pulled on his sweats, snagged the leash from its hook, and opened the front door, listening to the dog tap dance down the stairs of the apartment building into the predawn darkness.

Still cold, he noticed, his breath curling up into the light from the streetlamps.

"Stupid dog."

Karen was sitting at the kitchen table sorting vitamins and listening to the classical music station when he and the dog returned. He enjoyed some classical music, but he didn't know anything about it, so it was an uninformed pleasure. He opened the refrigerator, took out the grapefruit juice, and poured himself a glass.

"I'm going to have to quit eating pizza late at night," he said.

"You always say that," Karen reminded him.

He smiled, took a quick swallow of the juice, and grimaced at the taste. "Had the strangest dream. Must have been the pizza."

"What about?" she asked, shaking out two calcium-magnesium tablets into the small pile on the table.

"No idea," he admitted. "I can't remember."

She refused to begin a guessing game. "If it's important, it'll come back to you."

He nodded and sat down. Leafing through yesterday's mail and sipping juice from the glass, he came upon the latest edition of *Time.*

The magazine was his one concession to following current events, and he generally ignored much of the content, but this week's cover caught his eye. An angel, wings spread wide, graced the cover with printed promises of related articles tucked in a corner near the tip of one feathered wing.

"Look at that," he snorted, tossing the magazine over to his wife. "They got the wings all wrong."

His wife looked up at him suddenly. "How would you know?"

"Because I've . . . ," he closed his mouth with a snap, a sheepish expression on his face. "I was going to say, 'because I've seen one.' But that's not likely, is it?"

She shook her head.

He started to stand up.

The music on the radio was replaced with an announcer doing the morning news.

"There's more trouble in Bosnia, as Serbs, Croats, and Muslims continue to fight amongst themselves," the announcer droned.

"Trouble?" he asked, the juice glass forgotten in his hand, his eyes glazing over. *Trouble?* He felt the world lurch suddenly to one side, the table banging against his thigh. He thought he heard glass breaking.

A wave washed over him, and he went under. Can't see! Can't breathe! Don't let go! *he screamed, and the water filled his mouth.* Hang on! *Nothing to stand on, sand graining away beneath him. Cold. Like death, it was.*

"Jon Thomas!" his wife shook him, shouted in his face. "Answer me!"

He was sitting on the kitchen floor, leaning against a table leg. He'd dropped the juice glass, shards of it winking on the floor. The dog had retreated to her floor pillow.

"Broke the glass," he said, muzzily, starting to get up. "Better pick it up."

His wife pushed him back. "Jon, what happened? Are you OK?"

"'I'm fine. Why am I sitting on the floor?"

She shook her head. "I'm calling 9-1-1."

"No. I'm OK. What happened?"

She didn't answer. "You're going to the doctor. He'll tell us."

She started to get up, but he caught her arm. "No. Not sick. I'm not in pain." Then he giggled, "I've fallen, and I can't get up."

"That's not funny, mister!" she shouted in his face, balling her fist up in his sweatshirt. "You mumble something about 'trouble,' your eyes roll back in your head, and you fall on the floor! It's not funny!" She released her grip, her hand shaking.

"You're right," he nodded. "Not funny."

"Give me one good reason why I shouldn't have the paramedics here right now."

He was sweating and shaking too. And he wasn't sure that if he got to his feet he'd be able to stay there. But he knew he wasn't sick.

"For just a second, I was there," he said.

She was mystified. "Where?"

"Skip Day. My senior year in high school. The beach. The day we almost lost some people."

"Lost as in drowned?" she asked. He nodded. "You too?"

"Maybe," he answered with a shrug. "Some stuff I don't remember real well."

"So this is some kind of flashback?"

"Not the kind you're thinking of," he answered. "I never did drugs. Never even smoked. Something different, more like a dream," his eyes widened. "Like the dream I had last night."

J. T. managed to get into his chair. The dog, who skirted the broken glass and the grapefruit juice splattered on the floor, put her nose in his lap. He patted her head without thinking, but the faraway look stayed in his eyes. "This can't be happening," he moaned. "Not me."

"J. T., you're scaring me."

"I'm sorry, Karen," he said, stroking her arm. "I'm just not ready for this."

"Ready for what? You're not making sense."

J. T. took a deep breath. He still looked miserable. "Last night an angel came to me in a vision."

Karen blinked once and slowly slid to the floor beside his chair.

They both ended up calling in sick that morning. J. T. moved to the worn sofa in the living room. Karen joined him after she brewed herself a pot of peppermint herb tea. She brought J. T. a cup to be polite, but she knew he wouldn't drink it. He never did. He could be irritatingly stubborn about things like that.

He surprised her by sipping from the cup gratefully and falling back into the silence that he'd hidden in since the incident in the kitchen. With her hands wrapped around the warmth of her cup, Karen curled into a corner of the sofa and waited. Finally she spoke. "Tell me about this dream."

J. T. shuddered and took another sip of tea, his eyes coming back into focus. He'd been a long ways away just then. And it had not been a good place. "It's a little disjointed," he warned her. "Fragmented, like pieces of a broken mirror."

"We have the time."

"Do we?"

Fear washed over her. Not the controlled panic she'd felt when her husband had collapsed on the floor of the kitchen. That had been something here and now, something she could touch and move and do something about. This fear was seeing a thing she'd never seen in him before. She barely recognized his face for a moment. Then, just as suddenly, it was gone. And the story came out.

The Oregon Coast.
Midspring.
Skip Day for the senior class of Laurelwood Academy.

Ninety-four students accompanied by a dozen adult chaperones and sponsors.

1972.

———————————————

It rarely got really warm on the Oregon coast in spring. Today was no exception. A wind out of the south braced them. Pleasant enough, considering the possibilities of coastal weather. They wandered aimlessly, beachcombed, threw frisbees, played scrub football barefoot in the sand, built castles. As time ran on.

J. T. scrawled his initials and those of his junior class girlfriend in the sand, surrounded by a large heart shape. He lay down beside it, and a friend took his picture.

Later, that picture would be enlarged to poster size and would decorate his girlfriend's dormitory room. And they would break up when he went away to college. But for the moment, this picture, like everything else in his life, had the feeling of permanence, of rightness. This was the way it was meant to be.

He joined several of his friends as they ventured out into the water. So cold! The only thing colder was to get out soaking wet in the wind. In fits and starts, they waded out into deeper water, fully clothed, intent on body-surfing. J. T. never got the hang of it. The waves were wrong; he was wrong. He never figured it out, but he knew that he was among friends.

And then Sharon cried out, first in surprise, then in sudden fear, as she was swept out from among them. Wayne and Ken swam after her without even a thought and found themselves caught as well. But they kept going, determined to reach Sharon and hold her up between them.

In seconds, the warning began to pass. Janell and Kathy fought their way toward shore to get help, against the undertow they only now discovered. J. T. and his friend Dan stood their ground, sand leaching away under their feet, struggling to keep the others in sight.

Time slowed to a crawl. J. T. could see the waves coming in, bigger now as they inched out into the surf. He kept trying to get closer while keeping contact with the ground. Sharon's head bobbed to the top of a wave as it crested, and she disappeared behind it as it rolled on in at them. J. T. heard calls, frantic with fear from the shore. Adult voices, commands, and the sudden sounds of splashing as people rallied, led unerringly to the right place. A human chain was forming, stretching out into the surf, hands clasped with the strength of fright and love.

The hand that reached out to him was Wisbey's, the man who had been his father's dormitory dean many years before and gotten J. T. his part-time job in the factory. The strength in that hand had not lessened with the years, and J. T. was glad of it.

"We have to go farther out!" Dan called over the ocean roar.

The tall, spare young man began leading the rest of them out into the waves. J. T. was treading water now as the waves hit. He had a sudden irrational fear of losing his glasses in the water. A wave broke over them, and he went under, unable to get a breath before being buried in the murky green water. He gagged on the bitter taste, felt the hands that were holding him twist and burn in his own, and the terrible chill in his fingertips that told him he was reaching the limit of his strength.

The arms of his friends reached out, and together they gathered in the three lost ones. Gathered them in and pulled them back from the brink to the shore. As he and Dan waded out onto the sand, he saw Wayne heaving up seawater and saw Sharon bundled away to the fire, so cold she couldn't breathe. There was a blanket for him too. But he knew he'd done nothing except hold on—and that would become his guiding philosophy. But for now, the blanket was enough—and a friend to lean on when his knees gave out with no warning in the sand by the fire.

"That was a long time ago," Karen observed.

"Twenty-four years," he agreed. "It could have been yesterday."

"So what does that have to do with what happened this morning?"

J. T. drained the cup of tea, continued to hold it, running a finger around the rim.

"My friends are in trouble again," he answered.

"The angel told you that?"

He shook his head. "It wasn't like you think. It wasn't a conversation. It was . . ." his voice trailed off.

Light! So intense it seemed solid about him. The hand he raised instinctively to shield his eyes made no difference. He could see it behind closed eyelids. His stomach wrenched, and his head began to spin. Light so bright it hurt.

A place in the center of the bedroom where the light roiled, colors phasing and shifting. A place he could only see by not looking directly at it. A place where someone stood and spoke to him without words.

Karen took his trembling hand in her own while he tried to explain, falling silent finally in frustration. "It doesn't matter," she soothed. "It happened. That's all I need to know."

A tear squeezed out the corner of his left eye.

"What now?" she asked.

"My friends are in trouble. I have to help them."

"Like before?"

"Yes," he nodded. "Sort of like before."

J. T. looked her in the eyes, and Karen saw fear and misery in them as he remembered days gone by. But she also saw determination and resolve.

"I've got to help them," her husband muttered. "Or this time, maybe we'll drown."

2

LEAVING THINGS BEHIND

J. T. scanned the school yearbook.

David Eugene Turner, attended Laurelwood 1970-72, graduated from Livingstone Jr. Academy, Boys' Club Sergeant-at-Arms, ASB Spiritual Vice President, tenor in Concert Choir. Bequeaths a roll of masking tape to the guys in maintenance so they can fix anything.

He set the book down on the table and picked up the newspaper page he'd torn out. At the top of the page was the word "Obituary." Halfway down it read:

Clinton Eugene Turner, 1904-1997. The funeral for Clinton Eugene Turner, formerly of

Salem, will be held at 11:00 a.m. Monday, July 14, at Beck's
Funeral Home. Mr. Turner worked for many years at the Dole
Cannery after coming to Salem from the Dakotas, where he
worked on cattle ranches. His wife, Cora, preceded him in death
in 1989. He is survived by a son and daughter, five grandsons,
and a number of great-grandchildren. He was 93."

J. T. wondered how much he still remembered of Salem. He
hoped it would be enough to find Beck's funeral home . . . and
David Turner.

Grampa could fix anything with a roll of masking tape and a
few well-placed nails.

But he can't fix this, David Turner thought, sitting silently in the
church pew directly behind his parents. There were flowers at the
front of the room, around the casket. Carnations mostly, it appeared,
with some hyacinths thrown in for good measure. He could smell
them from his seat. Flowers weren't something Grampa had ever
given much thought to, generally. They were nice in their place, but
their place was rooted in the ground somewhere. Not here. But then,
Turner guessed, the flowers weren't really for Grampa, after all.

The pastor stood behind the lectern off to one side of the casket. As a young man, the pastor was trying mightily to speak with a
quiet dignity befitting the solemn occasion.

Turner thought the man would probably feel more at home
shooting hoops in someone's driveway.

"Our brother Clint is no longer with us," the pastor said.

Our brother Clint is dead, Turner amended.

Grampa had little use for euphemism. He was not a man to
sugarcoat anything. As a young man in Montana and the Dakotas,

he had ridden the rangelands on horseback and had paid the price for that kind of hard living.

Once his horse had spooked while he was dismounting. He'd caught his hand in a loop of the lariat hanging from the pommel of his saddle, and he'd lost most of one of his fingers. The healed stub of a finger had fascinated Turner as a boy, trying to think what it might have felt like to lose part of himself that way. But Turner would be much older before he actually understood.

Another time, Grampa fell from his horse and broke his arm. Alone, he'd been forced to catch his mount himself, ride a couple of hours to the nearest house with a phone, and wait there for the doctor, who came out from town and set his arm. The doctor told him to rest, and Grampa thanked him. When the doctor had gone, Grampa got on his horse and rode all the way back to the herd and finished his job.

A hard man in a hard land, he nonetheless had a sense of humor.

During World War I, he trained horses in Idaho for the military, and out of sheer boredom, he taught some of them to jump fences. He neglected to inform their riders, however, much to their chagrin and his amusement.

But it was not the stories of horses and riding in wild country that made the biggest impression on Turner. Grampa had taken him in to the Department of Motor Vehicles shortly after his sixteenth birthday so he could take his driver's test. He had failed the test because he hadn't managed to parallel park, and the failure humiliated him.

The next day, Grampa had taken him out to a quiet section of street in the neighborhood, found a parking space between two cars, then turned the wheel over to him. Quietly, with the same kind of patience he showed while working with horses, he taught Turner to parallel park. As he grew older, Turner often wished that he'd been able to tell the old man he loved him, instead of the dumb sort of gratitude that men showed one another. But it was a time when that just wasn't done, and as it turned out, Grampa had understood all along.

The congregation rose to sing a hymn, and his wife, Nancy, nudged him when he didn't stand at the appropriate time. She glanced at him, asking a question with her eyes.

He shook his head and shrugged, and she left him alone.

Gramma had died several years earlier of cancer, and when she died, the light went out of Grampa's life, and he began to falter. He became an old man right before their eyes. Turner had been off on his own by then, but on the few occasions he managed to return home, the difference was made even more striking because of his prolonged absence.

Turner began to notice the gray creeping into his parents' hair. Grampa's hair had always been silvery as far as he knew, but he remembered his mom's and dad's hair as dark black, which always amused him, since both he and his brother were blonde. But the gray was definitely there. He could see it now as they sat in front of him. When had that happened? His own hair hadn't begun to gray, though he had to admit, it did seem thinner than he remembered.

And suddenly it all caught up with him, and he realized he was having trouble breathing.

Turner excused himself quietly, sweat running cold down the back of his neck, and he left the service, desperate to get outside where he couldn't smell those hyacinths, afraid that he might somehow make a scene if he didn't get out of there. He found a side door out of the building and stumbled out into the sunshine. He ended up sitting at the foot of concrete steps leading out to the street on the side of the building away from the front entrance.

That was where J. T. found him.

"You OK?" his old friend asked.

Turner squinted up in the bright sunlight, not recognizing J. T. at first. "J. T.? Is that you?"

"Yeah. Are you OK?" he asked again.

Turner nodded. "Just had to get out of there, you know? Breathe some fresh air," he explained.

J. T. smiled and sat down on the steps beside him.

"How'd you get here?" Turner asked.

"I've been looking for you, and some of the others. I asked around. Heard about the funeral. Figured you'd come here."

"What's it been? Twenty years?"

"A bit more," J. T. said. "I'm sorry about your grandfather. I remember some of the stories you told about him, fixing stuff with masking tape, riding horses in Montana, stuff like that. He must have been a good man."

"He was my Grampa," Turner agreed.

"It's a hard thing," J. T. commented.

"I saw him just last Christmas," Turner said, falling back into the habits of friend talking with friend, as if the years had never come between them. "He was in a nursing home by then."

Turner had come home for the holidays, bringing his wife to meet the whole family for the first time. Grampa was failing rapidly, his Dad warned him. He might not even recognize him, but Turner had to see for himself.

The nursing home smelled of antiseptic and urine and something Turner couldn't quite put his finger on. Maybe it was the loss of hope. He was never quite sure. His grandfather lay in a hospital bed, the cold metal rails pulled up to keep him from falling out, from escaping.

"Dad?" his father said softly. "Look who's come to visit you, all the way from Montana."

Grampa was thin now, the skin of his cheeks hanging loose across the bones of his face. For a moment there was no sign of recognition.

Turner saw no spirit, no thought behind his Grampa's eyes, and even the body was finally abandoning the old man.

"It's Davey, Dad," his father prompted.

And just like that, the old man's face changed, the light flowed back into his eyes, and the slack, seamed skin took on life again. "I know who it is," the old man retorted. "How are you, boy?"

They had talked until he'd gotten tired and drifted off to sleep. It was the last time Turner had seen him alive.

J. T. listened without a word, nodding.

"There's something that just doesn't make sense to me about this whole thing,"

Turner said, rubbing his hands together in agitation.

"What's that?"

"What's the point of it all?" When J. T. said nothing, Turner went on hurriedly, as if his mind was shoving out the words faster than his mouth could handle them. "You remember my cousin Don, roomed with me my senior year at Laurelwood? Did you hear he died?"

"No."

"Cancer," Turner said, shaking his head. "He was seventeen. Almost no life at all. It doesn't make any sense. Grampa . . . he lived a long life, only to die half crazy at the end. Where's the sense in that? Where's the *dignity* in that?"

" 'Do not go gentle into that good night,' " J. T. said quietly.

"What?"

" 'Rage, rage against the dying of the light,' " he finished.

"What was that, some poem?"

J. T. nodded. "Something Dylan Thomas wrote, I think. He meant dying shouldn't be an easy thing, any time, anywhere. We should struggle against the darkness. Even if it wins in the end.

"Yeah, well . . ." Turner shrugged, about to say something, then falling silent.

J. T. stood abruptly, jammed his hands in his pants pockets, and turned to look down at his friend still sitting on the concrete steps.

"Remember the first time you fell in love?" he asked.

Turner nodded.

"You had her picture on your nightstand so you could look at her when you went to sleep and when you woke up. You got matching shirts; you went everywhere together; you even had cutesy little nicknames for each other. Remember how that felt?"

"I remember," Turner said, wondering where his friend was headed.

"Then you both graduated and went off to different colleges, and she found someone else."

"Yes."

"How did that make you feel?"

"It hurt."

"You bet it hurt. Big time, it hurt. And knowing what you know now, if you could, would you go back and change anything?"

Turner had to shake his head. The hurt was bad, but the love, as immature and fragile as it had been, was still a wonderful thing.

"Life hurts sometimes. But it's also marvelous sometimes. You can't really appreciate the one without the other. There will always be pain," J. T. said. "That's part of life. But there will always be joy too. And that makes everything worthwhile."

J. T. pulled a crumpled brown paper bag from his pants pocket and opened the top.

"In my family," he said, "we have a tradition when someone we love dies. We select something that reminds us of the person, the effect they had on us, and we put it in the casket as a remembrance. A way of letting go, I guess."

J. T. drew a fat roll of masking tape from the bag and handed it to Turner. Turner gasped in surprise, gripping the brand-new roll in both hands.

"I remembered the stories you used to tell. I thought maybe this would be some help to you," he finished.

Turner stood shakily, rubbing the tape with his fingers, the memories of his grandfather flooding over him.

"Besides," J. T. said, "he's not really dead. He lives in your memory . . . and God's."

Turner reached out and hugged his friend fiercely, choking back sudden tears. "Thank you," he managed. "I was drowning, you know?"

J. T. smiled. "Not while you have friends," he said.

The door at the side of the building above them opened, and Nancy peeped out. "Dave," she called, "the service is over. They need you now."

"Coming," he said.

"I'll see you in a bit," J. T. said. "We have lots to catch up on. Go on."

His friend turned and strode away, his hands back in his pockets. Turner climbed back up the stairs to his wife. "Who was that?" she asked.

"The best friend I've ever had," he said.

He joined the others at the casket where they waited to carry it out to the waiting hearse.

"You ready?" the pastor asked.

"I will be," he said, opening the lid one last time.

He placed the roll of masking tape carefully near Grampa's right hand. "Go with God, Grampa," he said, and closed the lid.

And when they lifted the casket, he was surprised to see how light it had become.

3

NOWHERE FAST

Who'd have believed it? J. T. thought.

He'd gotten thirsty driving home on I-5, taken an exit, and met an old schoolmate he'd never even thought of looking for. He flipped open the yearbook on the car seat beside him.

William Kelly, attended Laurelwood 1968-72, graduated Tualitin Valley Jr. Academy, Editor of the school newspaper, Assistant Editor of yearbook, nicknamed "Shakespeare," he is voted "most likely to write the great American novel."

Karen was never going to believe this.

J. T. started the car, pulled out of the parking spot, and headed back toward the Interstate and home.

"I-love-my-job. I-love-my-job," William Kelly chanted to himself.

He hated his job. From the time he walked into the kitchen in the midafternoon until the time he turned the key in the lock sometime in the early morning, he worked in a place that cut him at every turn.

"Whopper, Whopper-no-tomato, two large fries, and a six-piece Chicken Tender," he rattled off, turning away from the drive-through microphone as he keyed in the order on the cash register.

The order-taker behind him collected the money through the open window then passed the food back out. William heard the driver curse, then the car, a battered Ford with a University sticker in the window, screeched away. He glanced at the order taker, a high school student who had come in at the last minute to replace another worker who had called in "sick." Which meant "hungover."

"What was his problem?" he asked, referring to the customer who'd driven away.

"Thought he should've gotten his food faster."

"Maybe he'd rather have cold fries."

"Maybe he should eat at home," the girl observed. "Wouldn't hurt my feelings any."

William shrugged. "That's why they pay us the big bucks."

The girl smirked and traded places with him at the microphone. "Welcome to Burger King. How may I help you?"

He moved off, intent on getting more speed from the kitchen crew, who were understaffed and on edge already. After all, it was Saturday night and a full moon besides. The crazies were out, and many of them were drunk. They'd already had their share and more.

And the truth of it was, when he was really being honest with himself, standing outside the restaurant in the chill morning air after closing, watching the stars turn above him, he figured he deserved it.

A poor husband . . . a worse father—he had it coming. Sometimes he joked with the kids in the crew about having done something really awful in a past life to get stuck managing the Sannich Way Burger King. Mostly, they really thought he was joking.

"Hey, you! Burger King!"

He turned to face the front counter and a young man whose eyes said he wasn't seeing much of the real world at this particular time.

"How can I help you?"

"Look at this!" the customer snapped, hauling a white bag out for him to see. "You call this an order of onion rings? Look at this!"

William was many things, but he wasn't stupid. He had no intention of sticking his nose in the bag to see how many onion rings the guy had gotten. And he wasn't going to just lie down for the man either.

"If you'd like to purchase another order of onion rings, I'll be glad to help you," he said, looking the man in the eye.

"I oughta' kick your butt!"

William bent over just far enough to pick up the phone under the front counter and dial 9-1-1.

"Hey now, what 'chu doing?"

"Hello, police?" He ignored the customer. "Yes, I need an officer. A customer has just threatened me with physical violence, and I wish to press charges."

"Hey! Now just wait a minute, there. You can't do this. Don't need no police here. What 'chu doing?"

William fixed the man with his eyes again.

"You threatened me. And I'm calling the cops."

"You can't do that, man! You can't do that. I'm from Seattle!"

William almost laughed. "You might not want to be here when they show up," he advised. "They're on their way."

The young man cursed him soundly and left the store, moving none too steadily off down the street toward the downtown area. William took a deep breath and leaned against the wall. This was not the way he'd planned his life. Not even close.

He'd taught English back in the dim time, the time he remembered only by looking at old yearbooks and photo albums, because it had almost nothing to do with his present life. His wife had left him back then, driving away with the kids, her parents, and most of the furniture in her father's truck while he hid out in a motel a few miles away. After that, he slept on the couch, nursed the anger, and fought off nightmares.

The world stopped being what he thought it had been, and he saw that it could be cold and hard. That it often was. And when his downward slide slowed, he found himself managing a fast-food joint just down the street from the university where he used to teach. Once in awhile a kid would come along that reminded him what it was like to work with bright young minds just seeing the world for the first time. But they didn't stay long. Rarer still was the occasional customer who stopped being the thirty-second face to order a Whopper/no onions, large french fries, and a medium Coke and became someone real.

Tonight was one of those nights. The customer was a cab driver named Andrew. Always Andrew—never Andy or Drew. For a regular, Andrew was pretty formal about some things, William thought, but then maybe he had a right to be. Andrew often stopped in late on Saturday night, just before the dining room closed, and drank coffee. He'd talk with anyone about anything, and William found spending time with him worthwhile.

William leaned on his broom in the dining room and glanced over at Andrew, who sat in one of the booths playing solitaire and sipping coffee from a styrofoam cup. Like everything he did, Andrew played solitaire with a focused concentration that made it seem there was nothing else happening around him.

"The red eight goes on the black nine," William offered.

Andrew smiled and stroked his handlebar mustache, tapping the remainder of the deck against the tabletop with his other hand. "How's the fast-food business?" he grinned.

"Making the world safe for hamburger," William replied.

He slid into the seat opposite the older man. Andrew swept the cards aside and shuffled with quick, deft movements.

"You play?" Andrew asked.

William shook his head. "Learned solitaire when I was a kid. Played blackjack for matches, but never spent much time with cards. They weren't part of my fundamentalist upbringing. The church I grew up in didn't approve. The feeling was that playing cards was unsavory, associated with 'the wrong kind of people.' "

Andrew riffled the cards with an impressive dexterity that spoke of long association. "They have a point there," Andrew said. "Cards are just painted pieces of paper. The real danger is what you do with them."

"What else can you do with them? Besides gamble, I mean."

The older man grinned, showing a lot of teeth. "Funny you should ask." He fanned the cards out on the table. Selected a card here and there at random and turned them face up. "I've met people," he said, "who claimed to tell the future with cards."

"Just the sort of people I was talking about," William pointed out.

Andrew shook his head. "People can't tell the future with cards. Not your future, not their future. Nobody's. It's just a line. They do it for money and to get your mind off what they're really doing."

"Which is?"

"Reading your face, the way you move, stand, sit. The way you're dressed. Then they make guesses . . . sometimes very good guesses . . . based on what they've observed."

"And what do you see?"

"About you?"

William nodded. Andrew sat back, the smile gone from his face. "You're going nowhere," he said after a long pause.

William snorted. "Hey, don't sugarcoat it, tell me straight out." He started to get up, but Andrew waved him back to his seat.

"How long have I been coming here?" Andrew asked.

"About as long as I've been here," William answered. "Four, five years. Every Saturday night like clockwork."

"And I figure I know you about as well as any casual acquaintance might. Maybe better. Sometimes when the business is slow, like now, you let your guard down. Let yourself slip out and take a look around."

William didn't say anything.

"And when you do that, you don't like what you see. Do you?"

William looked away, staring at the traffic lights on the street outside, the rain a light mist that hung in the air. He shook his head.

"And yet each week, every Saturday night, you're here. How come?"

William almost didn't answer. But the temptation was too great. Someone had actually cared enough to ask.

"I've got nowhere else to go," he said, and closed his eyes. For just a moment he let the wall drop and looked at the pain he kept hidden behind it. It rose up in a towering wave that threatened to drown him, and frantically he slammed the wall back into place.

"Just bad luck, I guess," his laughter sounded nervous and uncertain even to him.

"Now there," Andrew said quickly, picking up the cards and shuffling with one hand, "is a whole other topic for discussion." He finished the shuffle then set the deck of cards in the center of the table. "Pick it up."

William picked the cards up, held them, feeling them still warm from Andrew's hands.

"Pick a card, but don't let me see it."

He obeyed then slid the card back in the deck.

"Now shuffle the cards."

His shuffle was awkward, the cards wanting to fly apart instead of into a neat arrangement. When he finished, he set the deck back on the table. Andrew picked them up, and they began to flow like water in his hands.

"Now . . . if I could show you the card you picked, would that be luck?"

"No, 'course not."

"Why?"

"It's a trick. You've done something that lets you know which card I chose."

"Good," Andrew said with a wide smile. "I was right, you're not dumb."

The older man began to sift through the deck, finally selecting four cards which he placed face down on the table without looking at them. "What are the chances that any of these cards is the card you selected?"

"Knowing you," William said, "I'd say the chances are pretty good that one of them is."

"But you'd be wrong." Andrew flipped over each card one by one—the King of Hearts, the King of Diamonds, the King of Clubs, and the King of Spades. "You see, I wasn't doing the trick you thought I was doing. There are some things in this life that you just don't know. There are some things in this life that are completely out of your control, some things you can't affect, even in a minimal way. You may think you can. You may think you know what's going on. And you may try to make things all work out. But it's a lot more complicated than it first appears. And you know what else?"

Off balance, surprised by Andrew's comments, William could

only say, "What?"

"It's not always your fault."

"What are you talking about?" Real fear began to show in William's voice.

Andrew looked straight into his eyes. "What happened in the past. Quit punishing yourself. Let . . . it . . . go."

"I don't understand."

"Yes, you do. Time to move on. Sometimes it's good to step out of life for a while, get your bearings. But you've been hiding here long enough."

William just stared as Andrew stood and headed toward the door. Searching for something to say, he picked up the cards and followed Andrew to the parking lot. Andrew opened the door to his cab and looked back.

"Goodbye, William."

"Goodbye? No more Saturday nights?"

Andrew shook his head. "Time for me to move on too. You think you're the only one wandering in the wilderness?"

He waved once as the older man pulled out of the parking lot. Lost in thought, he looked at the cards in his hand. Then behind him, he heard glass break and drunken laughter. "Wonderful," he muttered, turning to see four young men weaving up the sidewalk. One of them had just kicked the headlight out of a parked car.

"Hey!" he yelled. "Knock it off! I'm calling the cops!" he strode over to them, angry at their careless disregard, angry suddenly beyond his control.

One of them stepped forward to meet him and without warning punched him in the face. At the time, it didn't hurt all that much, he would later recall, but his head caromed off the brick wall of the restaurant, and his knees betrayed him. He crashed to the sidewalk, the cards littering the ground around him. He heard more laughter then the scuffle of shoes retreating quickly into the night. The next thing he knew, someone had leaned him up against the wall of the restaurant and was wiping the blood off his face with a handkerchief. Someone he knew.

"J. T.?" William asked.

"Yeah, it's me."

"How did . . . why . . . what are you doing here?" He pushed his old friend's hand away. He tried to stand up then had to accept J. T.'s arm for support.

"You got me. I just took the last exit off the Interstate and stopped in for a chocolate shake. I didn't know you worked here."

"Worked—past tense—is the operative word here."

J. T. shook his head. "Lucky I stopped, huh?"

William looked his friend in the eye. "Luck had nothing to do with it."

~~~~~~~

4

LOVE
LIKE A ROCK

J. T. picked up the phone and dialed a number from memory. While the phone on the other end rang once, twice, he paged through the yearbook on the table in front of him.

Gene Carver, attended Laurelwood 1972, transferred from Gem State Academy, winner of the Spring Thing Pie-Eating Contest, member of the Photography Club, the Environment Club, and the orchestra, bequeathes a slotted spoon to anyone working in the cafeteria who can guess the main ingredient of peanut-butter gravy.

"Gene? J. T. You want to get together for lunch this afternoon? . . . The Haven sounds fine. Twelve thirty . . . Hmmmm? Oh, just something I need to talk about with you."

"So . . . how's your daughter these days?"

Gene paused a moment, a french fry, liberally salted and ketchupped, halfway to his mouth. He glanced up at his friend J. T. sitting across the table from him then down again quickly at his plate. "Lindsey's fine . . . just fine," he said, looking up again.

J. T. sat there—his fork resting in his salad—leaning back in their regular booth by the window of The First Street Haven restaurant.

Like he has all day, Gene thought, *and he doesn't mind the wait.* "As far as I know," Gene added.

J. T. nodded, as if he'd expected that answer. "Been awhile since you've heard from her?"

"You could say that. About seventeen years! Yeah, I guess that qualifies as 'awhile.' "

Seventeen years.

When the divorce was final, Gene had watched the woman he'd married drive away with his year-old daughter Lindsey in a little white foreign import her father had given her. Gene, on the other hand, would be driving home in a rusted old Dodge that still had the marks of an ice-cream cone he'd bought for Lindsey. She'd gotten more of it on herself and the back seat of the car than she'd managed to get in her mouth. For just a moment, that memory made him feel warm. But the cold came back and settled in for good this time.

His father had put a hand on his shoulder, and his mother had turned to him, saying, "Someday she'll want to know who her father is, and she'll come find you."

He had clutched that hope to himself like a drowning man, desperate for something to hang onto, knowing even as he did so that his mother was hurting as much for him as he was hurting for himself. He forced himself to stand straighter and even managed a smile for her benefit.

"I know," he had said.

Unfortunately, they were both wrong.

"Are they still living in Kent?" J. T. asked.

Gene shook his head and set the glass of Coke back down on the table, consciously placing it back on the water-condensation ring it had made on the table between them. It was paying attention to the little things, he knew, that made it possible to get through the day without thinking too much about his life. But J. T. wouldn't let it go. "No, now they've moved to Spokane."

"Long ways to go."

"So what else is new?"

The divorce decree called it "rights of visitation." Every other weekend, every other holiday, a month in the summer. Just words, as it turned out. His ex-wife had taken his daughter and gone to live with her parents in Oregon, three hundred miles away.

Gene found he could only visit on an irregular basis, when he had the money to make the trip, and with child support on top of everything else, it wasn't often that he had the money.

"Do you call her, write her letters?"

"J. T., you want to drop this?"

His friend chewed a mouthful of lettuce thoughtfully before answering. "Can't do that, Gene."

"Why?"

"It's too important to let it lie."

Gene grimaced. "Well, you're going to have to. You're way out of line here."

J. T. nodded, agreeing, but refusing to back off. "I'm also your friend."

"There's a limit to how far you can take that friendship,"

Gene warned him.

"I'm willing to risk it," J. T. said.

Gene shoved the plate with his half-eaten lunch away. His appetite had vanished.

"If I were drowning," J. T. asked, "wouldn't you try to save me?"

"You're not drowning," Gene pointed out.

"No, but you are."

His former spouse had remarried two years after the divorce, and they had moved first to Kent then across the state to Spokane. Gene tried to stay in touch with phone calls when he could not go in person, with letters that his daughter couldn't quite read yet, with birthday and Christmas gifts sent by UPS so that Lindsey would know that, no matter what, he had not forgotten her. But it was never enough. His daughter grew so fast, changed so often, there was no way to keep up. Still he tried, and he kept on trying.

"Let me tell you about phone calls and writing letters," Gene snapped, angry heat flushing his face. "Lindsey's birthday was last month. I don't know how many department stores I wandered through, looking for something that would be the absolute perfect thing for her. And then I realized it wouldn't matter what I got her, because I had no idea who she was anymore."

He broke off and looked out the window at the cars passing by on First Street. J. T. waited.

"She never writes back. She never calls. I write . . . I call, but nothing comes back.

I send presents, cards, letters. I have to call to make sure she got them. I don't know who she is," he said again.

He had told J. T. that Lindsey never called. That was not strictly true. She had called him one time. About a week before a scheduled visitation, he had called to confirm things and learned that their phone had been disconnected. They had moved suddenly without telling anyone where they were going.

He went a little crazy.

And when his brain started working again, he picked up the phone and began dialing. He called his former wife's parents, who knew nothing he didn't already know.

He remembered the new husband's last name. It was unusual enough there might not be too many to call. He called everyone in Kent with that last name, happening on a relative who knew they'd moved to Spokane.

Spokane directory listed no one by that name. But he couldn't quit. He began to recall things from brief, polite conversations he'd had with the new husband. The man was an optometrist, Gene knew, so he called every business listed in the Spokane yellow pages, until he got the man's business and left a message begging for them to call and let him know what was going on. He had had to leave that message three times before his daughter, Lindsey, had returned his calls.

"Dad?"

"Lindsey? Is that you?"

"Yes, Dad. It's me."

"Are you all right? Where are you?"

"Everything's OK, Dad. We just had to move, and we didn't have time to call everybody."

"I was scared half to death, Lindsey! I'm your father! A phone call takes thirty seconds! I've been looking for you for five days now! When I called your house, the phone was disconnected. What's going on?"

"Mom's husband got a new job, and we had to move right away, that's all. Everything's fine. Mom will send you our new address as soon as we're settled in."

"But . . ."

"Gotta go, Dad."

"Yeah, but . . ."

"Bye, Dad. Just called to tell you."

"Bye, Lindsey," he said to a dead phone.

He continued writing letters, though he rarely called anymore after that. It was too hard to call and listen to the distance in the wires as he asked the polite questions about his daughter's life. Where was she going to school now? Did she have nice friends? Was she happy? How was the weather?

Sometimes it was easier if all he got was the answering machine. Easier for everybody. He gave up expecting any kind of response from her. The only time she wrote back to him was the time he'd gotten angry enough to lecture her about common courtesy and what people expected from her and her mother in terms of civilized behavior. Apparently, he'd struck a nerve.

"Dad," she had written, "If I don't write back to you, it's because I don't want to. Mother has nothing to do with it. And I don't want to hear anything like that again. Lindsey."

Giving up was easier than going crazy.

Gene had folded the letter carefully and put it in his wallet. Oddly enough, it was as close to his daughter as he'd managed to get in recent years, and he treasured it in a perverse sort of way.

He pulled the note from his wallet and handed it to J. T.

"That must have hurt," J. T. said, handing the note back, watching as Gene returned the dogeared piece of paper back to its safe place in his wallet.

"Used to," Gene admitted. "I don't feel much of anything now, really. Except maybe pride."

"Pride?"

"Yeah," Gene nodded as he swirled the melting ice in his soft drink. "She had the strength to stand up for herself and for someone she cared about."

"But you're her father."

"In name only, these days, it seems. But she's still my daughter."

J. T. scowled then. Gene recalled that J. T. and his wife had no children. His friend almost never talked about it, but he sensed some feeling down just below the surface and wondered if maybe he should say something to reassure his friend. J. T. didn't give him that chance.

"Someday, that's going to change, Gene."

Gene shook his head. "Inertia, J. T. Things in motion tend to continue moving. Things standing still usually stay still. Nothing's going to change."

J. T. surprised him then, reaching out, taking his left hand in his own with surprising strength.

"Someday!" J. T. hissed. "Everything's going to change! Everything!"

The look in his friend's eyes scared him. It was like looking at a stranger. But J. T. was no stranger. In high school, they'd waded out into the ocean and helped save three classmates from drowning. J. T. had stood with him at his wedding. They'd lifted weights together, gone out for pizza together, shared each other's lives. And Gene barely recognized him at this moment.

"Wait for it!" J. T. commanded him.

"O-OK, J. T., OK!" Gene stuttered back at him. "Are you all right?"

J. T. blinked, letting go of Gene's hand, and he was the way he'd always been. A little embarrassed, perhaps, but familiar once again. "Yeah," J. T. smiled as if he didn't know for sure where he was right then. "Yeah, I'm OK."

The rest of lunch went without incident. On the way out to their cars, J. T. clapped his hand on Gene's shoulder, just like his father had so long ago. "Don't give up hope. It's the only thing that keeps us from going down."

"Yeah, sure," Gene nodded, and wondered why he didn't feel much of anything anymore.

"Gene, I'm not going to let you drown."

J. T. left him standing in the parking lot beside his car and wondering what was going on.

That was why the phone call a week later took him by such complete surprise.

He was shifting produce in the warehouse, trying to make room for another delivery when the intercom called his name. "Gene, call one-zero. Gene, call ten."

That particular line accessed the information clerk in her booth near the front of the store. He left his hand truck loaded with boxes of lettuce and tomatoes and dialed the warehouse phone. "What's up, Judy?" he asked the clerk.

"Gene, there is someone here to see you. Real pretty. Says she's your daughter."

He almost dropped the phone. "Gene? You hear me?"

"Yeah . . . yes. Lindsey? Are you sure? Did she say what she's doing here?"

"No idea, Gene. What should I tell her?"

"I'll be right there," he said, suddenly worried. "Something must be really wrong," he muttered to himself.

He dashed out of the warehouse into the back of the sales floor, oblivious to the customers and the other employees. He was halfway to the front of the store before he remembered how long it had been since he'd last seen her, since she'd last seen him. Him in his dirty apron, carrying about fifty pounds too much around the middle, his hair beginning to thin seriously.

This was not the impression he wanted to make. This was not the way it was supposed to be at all. But he couldn't do anything about that now. She needed him.

Coming up from the side of the store, he saw her before she saw him. Standing there in the afternoon sunlight flooding the front windows of the store. Nearly as tall as he was, slender, with long hair flowing down her back, the same color as his. She clutched a heavy coat to herself as she waited for him, flipped her hair back with one hand, and he saw the flash of an earring. And a face he would never forget. She was beautiful.

"Lindsey?"

The girl turned at the sound of her name and he saw mirrored in his daughter's face his own concern that he did not measure up to her expectations.

"Dad?"

He hugged her to himself and discovered gratefully that she returned the hug even harder.

"I know this is kind of sudden. I didn't call ahead."

"That's OK," he reassured her.

"I just had to see you."

His mother's words and the strange words of his friend came back to him suddenly as he stood there hanging onto his daughter for dear life.

"I'm glad," he said finally. "I've been waiting for you."

5

GIFTS
OF THE SPIRIT

He'd come home from walking the dog one
evening soon after Thanksgiving and found Karen
crying. His yearbook was open on the couch beside her. J. T. glanced at the page and understood
why immediately.

"You miss Marie, don't you?" he asked.

She nodded and bit her lip.

"I miss Alan too," J. T. said. "And the girls.
Remember when Elizabeth was born and Alan's
car wouldn't start?"

Karen glanced up at him and almost smiled.
"Do you suppose they're still driving that heap?"

"I've known Alan McRory since
Laurelwood," J. T. remembered. "He was driving a '61 Oldsmobile even then, and he was nearly
always under it in an auto shop. It's even

mentioned in the yearbook. 'Most likely to change his own oil,' I think. He wouldn't know what to do with a new car."

"It's a good thing Marie wasn't the sort to be impressed by snazzy cars," Karen said. "Otherwise they'd never have gotten married."

"And they'd never have been such good neighbors," J. T. added.

Karen looked like she might start crying again.

"We have their new address, right?" he asked.

She nodded.

"Let's send them a Christmas card. Right now. Our first of the season."

"Our 'only' of the season," Karen retorted, but she was smiling.

Nearly closing time. Alan glanced up at the clock mounted on the back wall of the little drugstore. He got up slowly off his knees beside the display of facial tissue he'd just built. His right knee had been giving him some trouble lately. He didn't want to aggravate it, but it seemed like every time he turned around he had to kneel on the hard, tiled floor. He wasn't getting any younger, he guessed.

He walked past the shelves of ornaments and garlands and Christmas wrapping paper as he made his way to the warehouse. It wasn't much of a warehouse—more of a wide corridor behind the sales floor—but it was crammed with cardboard boxes filled with merchandise that would replace the Christmas stuff in a few more days.

Alan bumped into one of the pharmacists coming down from the break room, a tall man with his tie thrown over his shoulder to keep it out of his dinner. "Brig?" he asked the man. "Have you seen Don around?"

"Upstairs," the man answered. "He's working on the schedule."

"Don't tell me," Alan groaned.

"Yup. Corporate says we're open for Christmas."

Alan slumped against the wall. "It doesn't make any sense."

"I know," Brig said. "But they don't think like we do."

"They've got to have families . . . at least some of them," Alan protested. "They've got to understand what this means."

The big pharmacist shook his head. " 'Corp rats' only understand one thing. More money. If one thousand stores make five thousand dollars each per day, that's another five million dollars to throw at the bottom line."

"But it costs us that much to be open for the whole day!"

"You know that," Brig agreed, "and I know that. But they don't want to know that. They just slap each other on the back and look for someone to lay off."

Alan had been laid off before. He didn't like it. That was how he'd gotten here in the first place.

"And that's the real bottom line, isn't it?" Brig continued. "You want a job? Do what you're told. Work nights. Work weekends. Work holidays. And keep your mouth shut."

Alan had come to the little store just four months earlier after losing a job he'd held for eight years with another chain. He'd taken an interim job at a service station because he had a wife and two kids, and the work paid more than unemployment. He couldn't stand being on unemployment, whether he'd earned it or not. It was something he'd picked up from his father. An able-bodied man worked for a living—he didn't take handouts from the government. Even if it was his own money handed back to him.

He'd jumped at the chance to hire on with the drugstore chain. Decent, if not great pay—good benefits—excellent working conditions. There was only one drawback. Alan had to be willing to relocate . . . on a regular basis. That was how they'd come to the little community, drained financially and emotionally. The kids were going to be all right. Kids made friends quickly. He had his work. It was Marie he was worried about. They didn't know anyone here, and after paying the bills each month that accrued from the move, they were still worse than broke. Anything left after bills went for food, and they'd been eating a lot of potatoes these past few months.

"But, hey," Brig grinned, "work is it's own reward!"

"You're a sick man," Alan replied. "Guess I'd better go see the boss."

"Nobody's getting the day off," Brig warned, "not even the pharmacy, and with most of the doctors off duty in the whole area, we won't even be able to fill any new prescriptions."

"That's OK," Alan said, "I wasn't going to ask him for the day off."

He climbed the stairs to the break room and found Don, the assistant manager, in his little cubbyhole office chewing on a pencil and making occasional marks on a schedule sheet. When Alan appeared, Don took the pencil out of his mouth and began to tap the eraser end on the desktop.

"News travels fast," Don said. "Everybody's working. Even the Big Guy. No favorites."

"That wasn't what I was going to ask," Alan said, leaning against the wall.

There wasn't room in the office for another chair, so there was no place to sit. Don relaxed and stopped tapping the pencil on the desk. "So . . . what's up?"

This is going to be tough, Alan thought. "You know those artificial Christmas trees we've been using to decorate the store?"

"The little ones? The three-footers?"

"Yeah," Alan nodded. "I was wondering if it would be possible to borrow one of them, provided they don't sell before Christmas Day."

Don laid the pencil down on his desk. "Why would you want to borrow one of those trees?"

"It was a rough move, Don. We weren't expecting it to be so expensive. Frankly . . . we don't have enough money to buy a tree this year." Alan couldn't look at the other man. There wasn't going to be much of a Christmas. He and Marie had gone over the figures the night before. After the bills, there wouldn't be any money left for presents or decorations or even special foods. He guessed they were lucky they weren't on the street or living in a car.

Don didn't look happy.

"I'm sorry, Alan. If it were up to me, no problem. You could have one of the big ones, for that matter. But corporate policy says that nothing goes out the door that isn't paid for. We could both lose our jobs."

"That's OK, Don. I don't want that. It cost too much to get this job; I wouldn't do anything to jeopardize it or yours. I'm just trying everything I can to get my family some kind of Christmas. Thanks for your time."

"No harm in trying," Don answered. "Look . . . maybe I can get you out of here early enough to spend some time with your family."

"I appreciate that, Don. Whatever's fair."

Alan turned and hurried back down the stairs. He still had a few things to do before closing, and he'd just used up any spare time he might have had.

Alan washed his mouth out and hung the toothbrush in its place. Behind him, Marie brushed her hair in long, even strokes. The kids were already in bed, though he doubted they were asleep yet. It was not a happy household tonight. He'd had to tell them about working on Christmas Day. They seemed more upset about that than about his inability to get a Christmas tree. Marie was openly angry, though not at him. She wanted to complain to the company, but Alan had talked her out of it. He didn't think they could afford to "rock the boat."

They crawled into bed, and Marie settled into the crook of his arm. "I suppose it could be worse," she said.

Alan had trouble imagining anything worse, but he muttered a quiet agreement.

Marie went on. "I saw a homeless man today at the market holding a sign that said 'WILL WORK FOR FOOD.' "

"I've seen that, too," Alan admitted, realizing that things could be worse after all.

"At least we have a roof over our heads and enough to eat."

"That's OK for now," Marie said. "I understand about making sacrifices. But things are going to get better, right?"

Alan squeezed his wife. Her hair smelled clean and fresh from the shower. "Whatever it takes," he said. "Things are going to be better next year." She snuggled in close and relaxed against him. She was asleep long before he was that night.

Alan woke with a start, and for a few seconds, he had no idea where he was. He'd been dreaming, but now he was wide awake. The bedside clock glowed in dull red numbers: 3:57 a.m. He swung his feet out of bed, quietly, not wanting to wake Marie.

Bad enough that he couldn't sleep. No point in waking her too.

He slipped into his robe and padded down the hall, checking the kids' room. The soft light cast by the night light showed Alicia curled in a ball, sleeping just like her mother.

Elizabeth lay perfectly still on her back, her hands folded, looking up at the ceiling, wide awake. When she noticed Alan peeking in the open door, she sketched a half-hearted wave at him.

Alan came in quietly and sat on the floor next to his daughter's bed. "You're up kind of early," Alan whispered, "or late."

"You, too," his eleven-year-old answered in a hushed voice. Neither wanted to wake the younger girl.

"Did you have a bad dream?" he asked.

Elizabeth shook her head. "Just thinking," she said.

"Must be pretty important thoughts to be awake in the middle of the night. You want to talk about it?"

Elizabeth rolled over on her side to get as close as she could to her father. She held out her hand, and Alan took it in his.

"When we went shopping today—Mom and us—we saw a bum at the grocery store."

"She told me," Alan nodded, "but it's not polite to call him a 'bum.' He may be just like us, only something bad happened to him."

"Will something bad happen to us?" Elizabeth asked.

That's a really good question, Alan thought, but he kept his thoughts to himself.

Elizabeth had always been a worrier, like him, but she didn't need to deal with his insecurities too. "Why do you ask that?" he asked.

"Well, we had to move and leave all our friends behind. And it's almost Christmas, and you have to work, and we don't have money for presents and stuff."

"I see what you mean," Alan said. "Does seem like a lot of bad things, doesn't it?"

"I miss home."

Alan knew what she meant. "But we can look at all this another way. A long time ago, I had to move after I graduated from college in order to get to the city where I was going to work. If I hadn't moved to that city, I never would have met your mom. And I never would have had two beautiful daughters. It seemed bad at first, but it turned out pretty good."

"What about working on Christmas and not having any money?"

Alan sighed. She wasn't going to let go of this. "Well, I'll get paid extra for working on Christmas Day, and we could use the extra money. Maybe somewhere, someone will need us to be open for medicine or a last-minute gift for someone. I don't know about that. I'll have to leave that up to God. It's something I can't control, and I don't know anything about."

"Are we poor?" she wanted to know. "We don't have enough money for Christmas," she explained.

"It's true, we don't have as much money as we'd like," Alan agreed. "But we have what we need. You're sleeping in a warm house, even though it's raining out there. You had dinner."

"Potatoes," Elizabeth made a face in the dark.

Alan grinned at her. "I'll have you know that potatoes kept the whole Irish nation alive once upon a time."

"But we're not Irish."

Her dad laughed. "Scottish is close enough. Now that's enough worrying for one night. Time to catch a couple more winks. OK?"

Elizabeth nodded, and Alan pulled the covers up over his daughter's shoulders.

Alicia hadn't even stirred. He kissed Elizabeth on the cheek and slipped out the door.

Marie found him the next morning drinking a mug of cocoa and watching the sun come up behind the mountains in the distance.

"When did you get up?" she asked, running her hands through her tousled hair.

"Early," he said.

"Give me a taste."

Alan smiled and handed her the mug. She sipped from it and gave it back.

"Elizabeth was awake, worrying about stuff."

Marie shook her head. "She gets that from you, you know."

Alan knew that. "She was asking some pretty tough questions."

"Like what?"

"She told me about the homeless man at the market and wanted to know if something bad like that could happen to us."

Marie sat down beside him on the couch. The sun wasn't quite up yet, but daylight had turned everything light gray, and color was beginning to seep back into the world.

"What did you tell her?" she asked, helping herself to another sip of hot chocolate.

"I said that some things that look bad at first are really good things. She's just homesick, I think."

"You're getting pretty good at this 'Daddy' stuff," Marie said, then she got practical again. "I'll get the girls up and breakfast started while you shower."

"OK. I'll make their lunches while you get cleaned up."

She started to stand up. "Don't forget, a piece of fruit in each lunch."

"Alicia doesn't like apples."

"Too bad," Marie patted him on the hand. "She needs to eat right, and apples are what we have at the moment. Next time we'll get grapes for her."

Alan was halfway across the kitchen with his nearly empty mug of cocoa when he turned around, an odd look on his face. "Do you suppose that's how God does it?"

"Hmm?" his wife asked.

"You know. Does He give us stuff we don't like because He knows it's good for us?"

Marie thought for a moment. "I don't know. I guess so. He's a parent too. That would make sense to me. Now, get in the bathroom, or you'll have to share it."

Christmas Eve was a busy time at the store, and everybody was in a rush. Even so, Alan noticed that most people understood about long lines at the registers and sold-out merchandise. There was something special about the season. Retail was crazy, certainly, but people seemed to look inside and find the best parts of themselves, at least for the time being. He had even managed to find one last Holiday Barbie doll that had fallen behind some other merchandise on the shelf, and the customer had made a point of telling his boss how helpful he'd been.

Don let him know he'd done a good job and then asked him to help him for a minute with something special. He followed the man outside and around behind the store where everybody parked. There was a Christmas tree lying in the bed of his pickup truck.

"Where's your car?" Don asked.

Alan pointed out a root beer-colored Plymouth a couple of spaces away.

"You're a brave man," Don grinned. "That car's gotta be older than your kids."

"It's a classic," Alan laughed. "And it's paid for."

"So is this," Don said, picking up the tree and standing it up on the pavement.

"I don't understand," Alan said, his heart beginning to pound.

"You can't have Christmas without a tree," he handed it to Alan. "And just in case, we got some other stuff to take home to your family."

"But . . . where'd this come from?" Alan asked.

Don ignored the question. "It's tough moving into a new place, making friends," he said. "It takes a lot of money. Sometimes there's nothing left for the little things that make it worthwhile. There's decorations and lights and some food for the feast and a couple of little things for the wife and kids."

Alan felt his eyes fill up. He looked down for a minute, unsure of his voice. "Don, I . . . don't know what to say."

"Don't say anything. Just give me a hand with this stuff. It's heavy."

Alan picked up the two sacks Don had pointed out and helped him move everything to the trunk of his car. The scent from the tree filled the air around them. When they'd gotten the trunk lid secured, Alan straightened. "Thanks, Don. This means a lot to me, being able to give my family a good Christmas."

"I know," the man nodded. "I moved here once too. Just so you know, everybody helped out with this. They thought you should have a nice Christmas your first year here."

"It will be."

Alan, Marie, and the girls spent the evening decorating the tree. The girls were thrilled with the small packages addressed to them, and they spent several minutes shaking each one and guessing what it might contain. After things had settled down a bit, Marie handed him a Christmas card.

"This came in the mail today. Our first Christmas card in our new home."

Alan opened it and smiled.

"It's from Karen and J. T.," he said.

"Go ahead and read it," Marie prodded.

"Dear Alan, Marie, and girls," he began, "we miss having you around this Christmas, but wherever you might be, we wish you the best of times. You are not forgotten. Love, Karen & J. T."

"What was it you were wondering," Marie asked, "about God knowing what's good for us?"

"I guess I have my answer."

"I guess you do," Marie smiled.

Alan stood up and placed the Christmas card in the branches of the gift tree. It was going to be a great Christmas.

6

LAYING DOWN THE LAW

Davis Gregory was the sort of guy who could do no wrong, J. T. recalled. Nearly straight *A*'s at Laurelwood. The occasional *B*+ had saved him from being classified a nerd, without damaging his reputation for being pretty smart, overall. He could pitch a softball so fast that batters had feared him, particularly underclassmen, and with good reason. He had not been opposed to "brushing back" someone crowding the plate. And—which had never ceased to amaze J. T.—he had always had a date at school social functions, including the Sadie Hawkins event sponsored by the girls of Friendality Hall, Laurelwood's girls' dormitory.

That aura of good fortune had followed him on through college and out into the world, it seemed. That was his car in the parking lot. J. T.

was sure of it. A silver Lexus with the prestige license plates that read: "KIAI." So . . . what was Davis Gregory doing parked in an area of the courthouse parking lot reserved for people involved in criminal proceedings?

J. T. thought it might be worth hanging around to find out.

"Ladies and gentlemen of the jury," the judge addressed the four men and eight women seated against one side of the courtroom, "have you reached a verdict?"

"We have, your honor," Davis Gregory responded, standing in the front row of the jury box.

The bailiff crossed to him and accepted the sheets of paper that specified the charges against the defendant and the findings of the jury. In each case, under each specification, Davis, as presiding juror, had signed his name as required by the court. After three days of expert testimony, witnesses, and physical evidence, he and his fellow jurors had taken two and a half hours to reach a verdict. It was his first experience with jury duty, and though he felt they had done a good job, he could not help being uneasy, and he didn't know why.

The judge glanced quickly through the charges and specifications then looked up.

"Everything seems to be in order."

The prosecutor sat stiffly, waiting. The defender slouched in his chair in studied opposition to his opponent. Only the defendant looked at the jury, and Davis found, to his dismay, that he could not look the man in the face.

The judge proceeded to read the charges aloud: assault in the second degree, assault in the third degree, escape in the third degree, resisting arrest, and carrying a concealed weapon. In each case, he pronounced the verdict of "guilty," followed by the name of the presiding juror—Davis's name—signed below. The judge then polled the jury, calling them by name, to be certain that each juror agreed these were the correct findings. It was a long few minutes for Davis.

When at last the judge was satisfied, he thanked the men and women of the jury and dismissed them. The bailiff guided them out of the courtroom, and they picked up their coats and other belongings and left the courthouse through a back exit.

Davis stood for a moment outside the courthouse and breathed the cold January air, watching his breath drift away on the light breeze. He felt disconnected somehow, that while he and his fellow jurors had deliberated on the fate of one man charged with crimes by the state, the world had flowed on without them, without him.

"Davis?" said a voice as a hand came down on his shoulder.

He nearly jumped out of his skin.

"Sorry, Davis. I didn't mean to startle you."

"J. T.! No, that's OK. I just wasn't expecting it, I guess."

"Thinking deep thoughts again?" his friend teased.

For just a moment he was back in high school. That was where he and J. T. had met. J. T. had been the assistant editor for the school newspaper, and Davis had been a "sometimes" contributor. His friends often told him that he thought about things too much. That he thought too deeply. That despite the thinking, he often missed the point. It was an old joke, and J. T. was an old friend he hadn't seen in some time, though they lived in the same town. Their lives just didn't connect with each other.

"Maybe," Davis shrugged. "I just finished jury duty, and I'm feeling a little strange." He looked down at the ground as if searching for something at his feet, but he was really looking for the right words to explain his feelings to the other man.

J. T. nodded. "Judging people isn't easy."

"Something like that," Davis agreed. "That might be part of it, I suppose."

"What kind of trial was it?"

"An assault trial, mainly," Davis replied. "Some guy mixing it up with the police down on Front Street. There were weapons involved, so it turned out to be pretty serious even though no one was really hurt."

"You did your duty?"

"It was easy at first," Davis nodded, "and kind of fun. For three days we listened to the evidence from both sides. Like putting a jigsaw puzzle together. But then it got irritating. They kept moving us in and out of the courtroom, and we weren't allowed to talk about the case amongst ourselves even when we were alone. We ended up doing crossword puzzles together in the jury room just to fight the frustration."

The two men strolled through the courthouse parking lot, the winter sun glaring down from its low orbit just over the mountains to the south. As long as the sun was up, the day was warm enough, but when the sun dipped behind the mountain range, night would come on quickly, and so would the cold.

"But it's over now, right?" J. T. asked.

"Yes, we found the man guilty on all counts. Our part is over."

"But you're still feeling uneasy."

"*Um-hmm.* Having that much power over someone else's life. We just sent a man to prison for several years. We changed his life."

"Maybe," J. T. agreed. "It certainly changed yours."

"What?" Davis stopped beside his car.

"Life doesn't happen in a vacuum. Every action affects everyone around the action. Judgment affects the judge as well as the judged."

"Now who's thinking deep thoughts?" Davis chuckled.

J. T. smiled then changed the subject. "Listen, a bunch of us from the old days are going to get together on the coast later this summer. Sort of reminisce, get to know each other again."

"The coast? Where?"

"Remember where we went on Skip Day?"

Davis nodded, his mouth a sudden grim line. "I'd just as soon forget it if I could. Nobody should have been out in that water in the first place. We were all just lucky no one was drowned. No, thanks. Count me out."

The other man glanced away for a moment, and when he turned back, Davis caught a glimpse of the sun's cold light flashing off J. T.'s glasses. J. T. smiled and shook Davis's hand as he prepared to leave.

"Well, if you change your mind, give me a call. I'm in the book."

"Sure, J. T. It was good seeing you again. Say Hi to the wife and everybody."

As his friend walked off down the parking lot with his hands in his pockets, Davis slid behind the wheel of his Lexus. Thanks to jury duty, he had the rest of the day pretty much to himself. The boy was in school, his wife off at the community theater project, and he was at loose ends. Maybe a good workout would help get him back in synch with the rest of the world, he thought.

Davis knelt on the wooden practice floor, shaking from exertion, his breath coming in gasps. The back of his karate uniform stuck to him as it cooled, as he struggled to get his breathing under control. His teacher tossed him a towel, which he accepted gratefully with a silent bow.

"Your mind is not here," his teacher observed.

Davis nodded, still unsure of his voice.

"You go through the motions, but there is no joy."

"Joy?" Davis asked, surprised.

"You don't understand?" His teacher smiled. "I could explain, but it would be like a frog telling a tadpole about the sky. For now, the tadpole should just swim. Understanding will come in time."

"I'm not sure I even have the swimming down yet."

"You will," his teacher said. "Or you will drown."

Davis looked up, but the man had turned away and gone back to his own practice.

Whatever he had been hoping to accomplish by working out had not happened. His thoughts kept drifting back to the trial; he kept seeing the defendant, the look of hope draining from his eyes as the verdict was read. Even numb with fatigue, Davis could not shake free of that image. And his teacher had noticed.

He got to his feet, bowed, and left the practice floor headed for the showers. Maybe he could wash that picture away with hot water.

The shower soothed his body but not his mind. As he settled into the driver's seat of his car, he suddenly realized why. J. T. had been wrong. Judging people *was* easy. Davis did it every day; he'd done it all his life. Break the rules, pay the price. Everything was so simple. Or was it? How much had the lawyers *not* said?

His car phone rang, and he picked it up.

"Is this Mr. Davis Gregory?" asked a voice he didn't recognize.

"Yes, it is."

"Mr. Gregory, my name is Ted Grady, and I work as Security for the Valu-Price Store on the corner of Fifth and Washington. We have your son in custody for shoplifting. Could you come down and pick him up?"

A cold wash of disbelief swept over Davis as he sat in his car, clutching his phone. "Excuse me," Davis replied, "but did you say my son was arrested for shoplifting? Ryan?"

"No, sir, he hasn't been arrested. Just detained. We'd like to avoid involving the police unless it's necessary. If you can come down, we can release him into your custody, and the police won't have to be called. He doesn't have any prior record, does he?"

"No . . . no, of course not." Davis stammered. "I'll be right there."

He'd almost said that Ryan didn't have a record, that he was a good boy. But apparently that had changed. He sat there holding the dead phone in his hand. Then he shook himself, put the phone in its cradle, and entered traffic.

A few minutes later, Davis stood in rigid silence in a cluttered back office of the Valu-Price Store, listening to the man in charge of security tell what his son had done. Ryan sat slouched in a chair, his hands over his eyes, never once looking at his father. A couple of CDs lay on the security officer's desk among the paperwork.

"Your son claims that this was part of an initiation."

"Into what?" Davis managed to say.

The officer shrugged. "Happens all the time. You want to be part of the 'in' group, they demand you prove yourself. Put yourself on the line for them. Pretty common, really."

"Not in my family," he said through clenched teeth.

Ryan shuddered but didn't look up.

"He's free to go with you. All the paperwork's complete. As I said, you can expect to hear from my bosses within the month. He'll be fined, no doubt, but as a first offense, that will probably be it."

"Thank you, Mr. Grady," Davis said, extending his hand. "I appreciate your assistance."

The officer shook his hand, and Davis turned to his son. "Ryan, come with me."

Davis turned and walked away, listening as his son snatched his coat and backpack and hurried to catch up. Davis did not once look back as they walked out of the store. Ryan said nothing as Davis unlocked the door to the Lexus and let him in the passenger side. When Davis was seated behind the wheel, he put the key in the ignition, but his hand fell away, and they just sat there in the parking lot.

"Dad, I'm sorry," Ryan said finally in a whisper.

"About what?" Davis asked.

"You know, for the shoplifting thing."

Davis nodded. "Sorry for doing it, or sorry for getting caught?

Ryan didn't answer.

"I don't know what to say to you, Ryan. I had always assumed that you understood the difference between right and wrong."

"It was just a couple of CDs; the store wouldn't even have missed them."

"Wouldn't have missed them?" Davis asked incredulously. "Were they yours?" he demanded.

The boy shook his head, suddenly aware of the fury edging into his father's voice.

"You had the money for them the whole time. But you didn't pay for them. You stole them! You went in there to steal them. It wasn't just an impulsive thing. You planned it! It wasn't because you were hungry, and you stole something to eat. It wasn't because you had sick kids at home, and you stole medicine so they could get well. I wouldn't like that, but at least I could understand it. You didn't even steal them because you wanted them! You stole two CDs because your 'friends' wanted them."

Ryan didn't reply. He sat looking down at his feet, his hands knotted in his lap, his father's anger breaking over him like a tidal wave. "I didn't hurt anybody," Ryan muttered.

"Wrong again. You hurt your mother who will never be able to shop in this store without remembering what you did. You hurt me because I'm responsible for the members of my family, and I failed to teach you properly. But worst of all, you hurt yourself. You stole once. It'll be easier to do it again now."

"I won't do it again."

"I'd like to believe that. It's an easy thing to say, sitting here in the car with me. What's going to happen when you and your friends get together, and they tell you that since you got caught, it doesn't count, that you have to try again, to steal again. If you want to be friends with them."

Ryan glanced up guiltily.

"Where were your friends while you were being detained? Did they come in and tell the security officer that it was their fault? That they were responsible? No. They ran away. Not one of them stood up for you. Not one of them. And these are your friends?"

The boy began to sob, his face turned toward the car door. Davis felt the anger drain suddenly away. His son was hurting. He'd just realized that the people he thought were his friends had just been using him.

Without warning, J. T.'s words came back to him: "Judging people isn't easy."

Especially if he loved the person he was supposed to be judging. He'd put all his energies into this person, this person who'd made a mistake, who maybe deserved to be punished. But he loved Ryan too much, and he couldn't judge him . . . and maybe it was partly his fault too. Maybe, maybe, maybe. Davis covered his face with his hands. It was too much.

"Dad," Ryan said, his voice watery, "I'm sorry I stole that stuff."

"I know, Ryan," Davis replied. "I love you, Son. Too much to be your judge. I will always love you, whatever you do, whatever you become. But there are consequences to our actions. The more you grow up, the less I'll be able to help you with them. Eventually, it'll have to be *your* decisions. *Your* judgments."

Ryan nodded without looking up.

Davis turned the key in the ignition and started the car. "I guess it's time to go home," he said.

7

A SLEEP
AND A FORGETTING

with apologies to William Wordsworth

This wasn't like Tom, J. T. thought. Now he was worried. He flipped the yearbook open on the car seat beside him and found Tom's senior picture. It was something to do while he decided where to go from here.

Tom Jenkins, attended Laurelwood 1969-72, transferred from Auburn Academy, Legislative Vice-President of the ASB, Boys' Club President, Ski Club Treasurer, Student Week of Prayer speaker, graduating cum laude, voted most likely to "get a good education, get a good job, get married and have 2.5 children, and be a pillar of the community."

According to Tom's colleagues at work, he'd called in sick. They didn't have to say that his wife had left him just a couple of weeks earlier. J. T. knew that. They didn't have to say that Tom was taking it hard. J. T. could hear the concern in their voices over the phone. And they didn't have to say they were helpless. They worked with

Tom, but none of them were close friends. Getting involved might be awkward. But Tom *was* J. T.'s friend, and *he* could do something about it.

Just like last night and the night before, the dark man came to him. Slipped out from behind the curtains as if he'd been hiding there all along, moved across the darkened bedroom, stood at the foot of Tom Jenkins's bed and waited, a walking shadow come to rest. Tom lay in the bed and watched him, a darker figure in a blackened room, and knew beyond a shadow of a doubt that the dark man was bad. Very bad.

It was a dream, Tom knew. Of course, it was a dream. Had to be. It had been a dream last night and the night before. And just like those other times, Tom struggled to move and cry out at this intruder. All that came out was a strangled moan as he twisted in the bedsheets. And the dark man just stood there, looming over him at the foot of the bed, a figure of silent menace.

And then it was just an empty room, a darkened bedroom in an empty double-wide mobile home. Tom reached out with his right hand to touch Cindy's arm, and his hand hit cold bedsheets on that side of the bed.

"Oh yeah," he gasped, the dream fear beginning to leak out of him. "Forgot."

He untangled the sheets and stumbled in the dark into the bathroom adjoining the master bedroom. His hand on the light switch banished the remaining shadows in a burst of light so bright it hurt.

All those lights, he thought, as he stood there in front of the sink, squinting at his reflection in the mirror, waiting for his eyes to adjust to the light. *Three hundred watts in each one.* Cindy hadn't wanted any shadows when she was putting on her makeup. He had joked about getting sunburn, but by that time, she hadn't been laughing at his jokes. No shadows in the bathroom . . . no, sir. Just the one in the bedroom every night, coming for him.

He twisted the taps on the faucets, cupped cold water in his hands, and noticed they were shaking just before he splashed the water in his face. It hurt. So he did it again. It was a way of proving he was still alive. When he looked at himself in the mirror again, he was in better control. He ran wet fingers through black hair, saw the circles under his eyes with an almost clinical detachment.

Now he could go back to bed. He wouldn't sleep. He'd done this before, and he knew how it went. But at least the dark man wouldn't be back. He only came when Tom was asleep, and Tom knew that he'd be awake the rest of the night. Remembering.

Because like the lights and the cold water, remembering hurt.

Next morning the doorbell snapped him out of a light doze. He'd fallen asleep with the television tuned to Regis and Kathi Lee, slumped down on the couch. He hurt all over from the awkward position, and it took several seconds to collect himself. The doorbell rang again before he could answer it, and he was about to tell the salesman to shove off, when he realized that he knew the person standing on his front walk.

"J. T.?"

"Tom. I called where you work, and they said you'd called in sick. They seemed concerned, so I thought I'd come out and check up on you."

Tom squinted at the sunlight and began to realize what he must look like to an old school friend like J. T. Hair wild from a fitful sleep, gray stubble of a beard he hadn't shaved that morning, the wrinkled white T-shirt he'd slept in, and baggy jogging pants hanging on a gaunt frame. He could just about bet what his friend was seeing.

"You going to ask me in, Tom?" J. T. asked.

He'd been staring at J. T., not seeing him really, but J. T.'s question brought him out of it. "Yeah, sorry. I'm having some trouble . . . adjusting . . . to things," he admitted, ushering the man into his home, a home that looked just like it had when Cindy had walked out of it with her father two weeks, three days, and thirteen hours ago.

Tom waved J. T. to a seat on the couch he'd just vacated then remembered enough of his duties as host to rummage in the kitchen for something to offer his visitor. The refrigerator was nearly bare, except for a six-pack of cheap cola. J. T. passed on the cola, but Tom pulled the tab on one can and took a swallow that brought tears to his eyes.

"I heard about Cindy, Tom," J. T. began. "If there's anything I can do to help, I want you to know I'm just a phone call away."

Tom shrugged and took another swallow from the can of soda.

"Are you getting enough sleep?" J. T. asked.

"Um . . . no," he answered. "Don't want to sleep. Can't. Not anymore."

"How much of that stuff have you been drinking lately?" he asked pointedly.

"Too much. Not enough. Couldn't tell you. It keeps me awake, and it tastes really bad. What more could I want?" Tom shrugged again.

J. T. leaned forward from his seat on the couch and looked hard at Tom. Then he nodded, as if he'd come to some kind of agreement with himself. "Take a shower and get dressed," he said. "I'm taking you out for breakfast. There's something I want to talk to you about."

Tom made a weak attempt at refusal, but J. T. would have none of it. He found himself, despite his initial foot-dragging, pulling into a Denny's parking lot, his hair still damp from the shower, dressed in clean, if wrinkled, clothes.

On the ride over, he'd protested about not feeling hungry, but when he and J. T. walked into the restaurant, the smells of cooking food washed over him, and his stomach growled loud enough he was sure his friend could hear. His knees went rubbery, and he was glad to get a table quickly so he could sit and hide the shaking. He ordered a cheese omelette with chili poured liberally over it, a side of hash browns and toast, and a large glass of grapefruit juice. J. T. settled for a pecan waffle with judicious amounts of maple syrup and butter and an orange juice. He was almost sick with need by the time the food arrived, and for several minutes neither of them said anything as the food rapidly disappeared.

J. T. seemed pleased that the idea for breakfast out had been such a success. Tom rewarded his friend with a satisfied smile as he set down the empty glass of juice. J. T. had made short work of his own breakfast, Tom noticed, and they were just sitting now, enjoying the ambiance of a busy place filled with good smells.

"Thanks, J. T. It's been a while since I've eaten this well."

J. T. nodded acceptance. "That's what friends are for. I should have gotten together with you sooner. When I first heard that Cindy had gone away. I just wasn't sure it was appropriate to barge in on you."

"I'm glad you came."

"Your friends at work are worried."

Tom dropped his eyes. "I've been having difficulty concentrating on work."

"Only natural," J. T. said, "considering. But this looks like more than just 'trouble concentrating.' Forgive me, but you look ill."

"Part of that's not eating," Tom agreed. "The rest is not sleeping."

"Have you seen a doctor?"

Tom paused for just a moment, wondering if J. T. would think he was crazy.

Maybe I am, he thought. "A doctor can't help me with the dark man."

J. T. sat up suddenly, leaned forward, and dropped his hands in his lap. He said nothing, but he seemed to be listening with his entire body.

Tom went on. "He comes to me every night while I'm sleeping. Slips out from behind the curtains and stands at the foot of the bed," he explained, his voice tight in his throat. "He's like a black hole. He's darker even than a dark bedroom at night. No light escapes; he sucks it in around him as he moves. And he's coming for me. So far I've managed to wake up."

"Then he's a dream."

Tom nodded as if that were obvious. "But there's more to it than that. I can feel him in the darkness. I'm terrified of him. I can't escape him. He comes for me every night."

"When did this start?"

"The night Cindy's father came and took her away."

J. T. seemed interested in Tom's choice of words, but he said nothing about that.

Instead, he asked if there was something Tom knew that he wasn't telling. Tom nodded.

"I know who he is."

"The dark man?"

"Yes. I can't see his face, but I've always known. It's Cindy's father."

J. T. paid for breakfast, left a tip, and the two stepped outside the restaurant. Instead of going to the car, though, J. T. set off down the sidewalk. Tom hurried to catch up. "I like to walk my breakfast off when I get the chance. And it's a good day for it. Besides, I thought it might be easier for you to talk and walk at the same time. I think better in motion."

Tom smiled, stuck his hands in his pants pockets, and noticed for the first time that the sunlight was a wonderful thing.

"You and your father-in-law didn't get along, huh?" J. T. prodded after a couple minutes of small talk.

"Understatement. We pretty much despised each other. Didn't start out that way, though."

"Tell me about it," J. T. suggested.

"We could never get away from them—Cindy's parents, I mean. I should have seen the handwriting on the wall when they had us cut our honeymoon short without warning so they could help us move into our new apartment and then made all the decisions about what went where. Every weekend they drove up to visit. Every day they called. Saying it now just sounds like sour grapes, and maybe it is a bit, but we never had a chance to be just "us." With people our own age. They were always there! I took a job farther away, and it slowed down the visits a little, but they never stopped. And it got even worse when Cindy got pregnant. Suddenly, her mother was living with us for weeks at a time."

For just a moment the pain was so great that Tom stumbled, and J. T. caught him with a hand on his shoulder. "When Cindy lost the baby, she began to cling to her parents even more, especially her father. She needed his approval. And she wouldn't take it from me. We were both hurting so much, we couldn't seem to help each other with the pain. We had named the baby, see . . . and we . . . we never even got to hold him, you know?"

The tears cut coldly down Tom's face as the memories gripped him. J. T. steered him into a local park and sat him down on a park bench and waited for him to recover.

"You're a good friend, J. T.," Tom finally gasped out.

"We'll see," J. T. said. "There's more, isn't there?"

Tom nodded, unconsciously wringing his hands. "During their last visit, things got out of hand. Cindy's father made some kind of remark about me not taking good enough care of his daughter. I stood up and opened my mouth to order him out of my house, but I never got the chance."

"He hit you?" J. T. prompted.

"More like grabbed me and shoved me back down in my chair. Told me if I said one word, he'd rip my head off." Tom paused, choosing words carefully. "I never solved my problems with my fists, J. T., never. I couldn't even speak. All I could do was sit there with him standing over me, his hate just dripping out of him on me. Finally, he stood back, collected his wife and his daughter, and he left. That was two weeks ago."

"And the dark man appeared to you that night?"

Tom nodded. "You know I filed as a conscientious objector during the Vietnam War? *I couldn't take a life,* I thought. I was wrong, J. T. If I'd had a gun that night, I'd have shot that man."

J. T. stuck his hands in his pockets, jingled the loose change, and paced back and forth in front of Tom, who sat dejectedly on the park bench, his elbows resting on his knees.

"Remember back in high school," Tom mused, "back when our class went to the beach?"

J. T. turned slowly and looked him in the eyes. He nodded but said nothing.

"I feel like I did then . . . afraid I'm going to drown or that someone I care about will. Only this time, someone did. And I can't seem to get back to shore. You know? Am I making any sense at all?"

His friend said nothing at first, just held out his hand. When Tom reached out and took it, J. T. smiled fiercely. "You won't drown," J. T. said. "I won't let you."

That night as Tom pulled the covers up around his neck, J. T. settled down in a big overstuffed chair he'd dragged into the room next to the night stand. "You sure you want to do this?" Tom asked.

"What are friends for?" J. T. answered.

"I haven't had anybody watch over me since I was a boy with rheumatic fever. Feels kind of silly now."

"Nothing silly about one friend helping another," J. T. said, pulling a comforter up around his shoulders. "Now, shut up and go to sleep."

Tom reached over to the light on the night stand, clicked it off, and for the first time in two weeks, he felt at ease with going to sleep.

The window curtains parted noiselessly, and the dark man stepped through. Tom watched him come across the floor toward the bed and felt a wave of fear crash over him. He opened his mouth to scream, and suddenly the bedside light went on. The dark man straightened then shredded, before his eyes, the light, tearing him apart in one overwhelming pulse.

"You OK?" J. T. asked, taking his hand from the lamp on the night stand.

Tom gulped in air and nodded. "Did you see him?" he asked, the line between dream and reality no longer clearly drawn.

J. T. shook his head. "No," he said. "There was no one here to see, except you."

"All a dream," Tom told himself again, trying to convince himself.

J. T. rubbed his eyes with his fingers. "More than a dream, Tom," he said. "You can't escape the dark man, and I think I know why. The dark man is in you. He's part of you."

"No, I told you who he is."

J. T. shook his head again, his eyes red with fatigue. "As long as you hate him, you are bound to him . . . even tighter than you were bound to Cindy by your love. Most people don't know how to love, but we all know how to hate, and until you can let go of that hate, let go of Cindy's father, you will keep dragging him into your bedroom at night."

"What?"

"You talk in your sleep. Did you know that? I didn't catch it all;

you ramble and mumble. But I heard you call him."

"But why?"

"I don't know. Maybe to relive the pain, maybe to fuel your hatred with fear. I don't know. I'm not a psychologist, and I'm not a pastor, but I know one thing for certain."

Tom shivered. He wasn't sure he wanted to hear anything more.

"Someday, you're going to have to forgive Cindy and her father and let them go if you ever want to be free."

He shook his head sadly. "I'm not sure I can do that."

"I'm not sure you can either," J. T. said. "I'm not sure I could do it in your place."

J. T. leaned forward, his elbows on his knees, and spoke without looking up. "It's probably the hardest thing you'll ever have to do, and it won't be done tonight. You're looking at some serious, long-term effort. And you're going to need more help than I can give you."

J. T. wrapped the comforter around his shoulders and left the bedroom, dragging part of the blanket on the floor behind him. Tom sat in the middle of a big, empty bed, the blankets twisted in his hands, staring down the hall after J. T.

For the first time in longer than he could remember, Tom began to pray.

8

REMEMBER
WHEN

"You got your wool socks?" Karen asked J. T.

"Yup, got 'em."

"And your toothbrush?"

"*Mmmhm.* Got everything."

Karen didn't believe him.

"Anything I forget I can do without for two or three days," J. T. objected. His wife gave him a knowing look, and he gave up. He hugged her and kissed her on the forehead. "I wish you were coming," he said. "The San Juans are beautiful this time of year."

"Give Mike and Ann my love. I'll see them next time."

"OK," J. T. said as he closed the door behind him and went down the stairs to the car.

Karen sat down on the couch and picked up

her cup of herbal tea. J. T.'s yearbook lay open on the end table. She slid it on her lap and paged through it.

Mike Anthony, attended Laurelwood 1970-72, graduated from Laurelwood Elementary, ASB President, Boys' Club Vice-President, Student Council member, Ushers' Club, Physics Club, contributor to school newspaper and yearbook, Mission Outreach organizer, graduated summa cum laude, voted "most likely to change the world."

Karen set her tea down and closed the yearbook. "I wonder if he remembered to take his razor." Then she got up and started making herself some lunch.

Mike Anthony stood in the galley of the little twenty-eight foot San Juan hull sailboat and futzed with the stove. J. T. was late, but Mike knew that if he began making hot chocolate, someone would stop and interrupt him. It always worked that way. Some kind of universal law, he guessed, on the order of "a watched pot never boils." An eagerly awaited former roommate never appears, Mike formulated, unless one is making cocoa or figuring pi out to ten decimals.

A pair of white deck shoes went by the starboard porthole as he was stirring in the gourmet cocoa mix, and after a couple seconds he heard a familiar voice. "Anybody on board?"

Mike turned the stove down low so the cocoa wouldn't scorch and stuck his head out the hatch of the cabin. He took one look and snorted with laughter. J. T. wore white deck shoes, white bell-bottomed pants, a long-sleeved red knit shirt, and a sailor's cap with the brim inverted. Anyone who had watched television in the sixties or seventies would have recognized the Gilligan outfit, and to top it off, J. T. was wearing Groucho Marx nose glasses.

"What do we do now, Skipper?" J. T. mimicked Gilligan's famous whine.

"You look pretty silly, J. T.," Mike observed with a grin.

J. T. grinned back, slipping off the Groucho glasses.

"That was the idea," he said. "Is that hot chocolate I smell?"

"Yup," Mike replied, waving his long-awaited friend on board, "I made enough for two."

J. T. stepped gingerly from the dock across the gunwale of the sailboat and into the cockpit, the Groucho glasses in one hand and a duffel bag in the other. The sailboat rocked a little to starboard as he stepped aboard, and although Mike made the necessary adjustment almost unconsciously, J. T. had to make an obvious effort to maintain his balance.

"Haven't spent much time on the water, have you?" Mike asked.

"It's that obvious?"

Mike nodded. "That's OK; I won't send you aloft."

"Aloft?" J. T. glanced upward at the slim metal mast, uncertainty plain on his face.

"Gotcha."

J. T. grinned at himself. "I was wondering how long it would take for the Merry Prankster of Sittner Hall to appear. Where's Ann?"

"Ann isn't coming," Mike said, taking J. T.'s duffel bag. "She's got a medical seminar this weekend."

"Karen couldn't come either. She had to work this weekend."

"Looks like it's just you and me. Come below and I'll show you where everything goes."

A few minutes later, they cast off the lines and motored gently away from the dock in Friday Harbor and out into the San Juan Channel. Day died softly about them as they sat in the cockpit drinking the last of their hot chocolate, talking quietly, and watching the lights along the shoreline come on. It was Good Friday, and though the skies were lightly overcast, there was no threat of rain, and the moon shone brightly.

Mike watched the tension ease out of J. T. as he sat across from him holding the cooling mug of cocoa in both hands. It was always like this, he thought. Even people who didn't sail began to relax on board. Maybe it was the enforced idleness. Not too many places to go on board a small sailboat underway. But Mike guessed it had something more to do with the slap of water against the hull, the light breeze in the rigging.

He planned to motor down the Channel until they reached Cattle Point to the south and open water. Then he would shut down the little outboard engine, and they would sail in comparative silence.

"In the dark?" J. T. asked.

Mike nodded. "Good clear night. Plenty of navigational beacons. We shouldn't have any problem, and sailing at night is kind of special."

J. T. had unfolded the nautical map of the San Juan Islands, and Mike pointed out their destination for the night, a little cove up behind Charles Island to the east of Cattle Point.

"What's this," his friend asked, indicating a point on the map. "It says 'Bomb.' "

"Oh, that," Mike grinned. "Nothing to worry about. The navy installation on Whidbey Island uses that area for live ammunition practice. That's just a warning to the public not to drop anchor or fish there. Hard to say what's down there. We won't be going that far south."

"You're not kidding, are you?"

Mike shook his head. "I wouldn't dare make up something like that. Truth is always stranger than fiction. Why . . . don't you trust me?"

"You noticed I waited for you to drink your cocoa first."

Mike smiled. "A little paranoid?"

"You forget. I've known you since Laurelwood, and I roomed with you in college.

Remember when you bought that dirt bike that one winter and rebuilt it in our room?"

He'd forgotten about that. It made him smile again.

"Do you recall how you tested it out once you were finished?"

"Sure. I rode it around on first floor, until the dean came down."

"I was taking a shower at the time," J. T. reminded him. "I stepped out into the hall afterward and nearly got run down by the thing!"

"It was snowing outside. You couldn't have expected me to go outside with it."

"That was the problem, all right. Nobody could count on you to do what was 'expected.' You were always a little on the edge."

"I like it on the edge," Mike agreed, downing the last of the cocoa and setting his mug in a basket where it wouldn't slide around and get in the way. "That's how I got where I am today."

The question is, Mike thought to himself, *where exactly is that?*

Cattle Point fell farther behind them as Mike brought the sailboat about, the sail "luffing" as the boom swung across the cockpit. He turned the tiller over to J. T. while he trimmed the sail to take full advantage of the breeze. Even though it was spring in the San Juans, both of them had put on coats and stocking caps. Mike had taught J. T. how to recognize the different beacons and read the nautical map so he could tell his approximate location, even in the dark.

They had been playing "remember when" the entire time, reliving the years since Laurelwood, when they had roomed together at Walla Walla College, "the place so nice, they named it twice," Mike recalled. They'd remembered the giant water balloon slingshot they'd made out of surgical tubing and a plastic funnel, the one they'd used to pelt the outfielders playing softball in the ball fields behind the dorm. It had been confiscated after they'd lobbed a water balloon over the library, across the street, and through the front window of Conard Hall, the women's dorm.

They remembered the time someone set fire to the outside dumpster behind Sittner Hall, the men's dorm, and they'd been wakened to the sounds of firetruck engines, strobing emergency lights, and the sounds of hairspray and deodorant spray cans cooking off inside the metal container. Water fights and shaving cream raids in the middle of the night, listening to the church bells toll the hour across the quiet eastern Washington community, the chatter of fellow students in the cafeteria at mealtime, the gritty taste of dust in the air from one of the infrequent windstorms. It all came flowing back to them, the memories taking on the special glow reserved for good times and good people.

"I lost track of you when you spent that year in Rwanda," J. T. mentioned.

Mike's rueful expression caught his former roommate's attention.

"What happened over there?"

"I was too naive," he answered. "I went over there thinking I could accomplish great things. 'Student missionary!' Sounds pretty grandiose, come to think of it. I spent most of that year babying an ancient generator that powered the compound."

"Could have been worse," J. T. said. "They could have asked you to preach."

Mike snorted. "They did . . . once. The translator said I was too boring." He shook his head. "And I did such a lot of good while I was there. Changed everything for the better."

The sarcasm was a discordant note out of tune with the sound of waves against the bow and the pop of the canvas.

"Just last year the Hutus and the Tutsis decided they didn't like how the country was being run, so they took out their machetes and hacked each other into bloody little pieces."

J. T. shook his head, and Mike could see him remembering the same news stories he'd watched with growing horror as the Rwandan government dissolved in terror and blood, and refugees flooded the surrounding countries of Africa.

"Remember when we thought we could make a difference?"

Early morning crept up on the little sailboat anchored in the quiet water of the cove. Mike moved quietly from the cabin where J. T. was still asleep into the cockpit where he could stretch and look around. It was light, but the sun hadn't come up yet. The water was a silver mirror all about them, and birdsong from the shore was the only real sound. Mike went up to the bow and sat cross-legged just in front of the cabin. This was his favorite time.

On the opposite side of the cove, a derelict swung at anchor. Stripped of everything valuable, the hulk was a floating collection of rusted metal, an eyesore clashing with the early morning beauty. Mike had known it was there when they came into the cove the night before, but it had been invisible in the darkness, so he'd given it a wide berth. Watching it as the sun came up behind him, warming his back and shoulders, Mike studied the floating wreck, wondering if it was a fitting symbol of his life.

J. T. had slept restlessly at first, after remaking the bunk bed Mike had short-sheeted for his friend. Sometimes, Mike knew, sleeping in a new place like the restricted space of a sailboat bunk did that to a person. But Mike didn't think that was it. His friend had accidentally wakened him in the early morning darkness, mumbling something about "drowning." Afterward, his breathing had become regular again.

The forward hatch of the cabin popped open behind him, and J. T. stuck his head up, his hair still tousled from sleep. "You snore," he said.

"You talk in your sleep," Mike replied without turning around.

It was an old ritual. Mike's snoring was legendary. In college, J. T. claimed that Mike had routinely rattled the windows of the dorm room. Fortunately, J. T. slept soundly once he actually got to sleep, though, as Mike had pointed out, he talked from time to time. Once Mike had held a brief conversation with him in the dark only to find out the next morning that J. T. remembered nothing about it.

J. T. ran his fingers through his hair and looked about. "Where'd that come from?" J. T. asked, nodding toward the derelict.

"Just one of the local hazards the maps don't mention."

"I didn't even notice it last night."

"I knew it was here. That's why we're on this side of the cove. But it does sort of draw your attention, doesn't it?"

"All this beauty," J. T. muttered, "and that's the first thing we see. Interesting."

"Pretty hard to ignore," Mike shrugged. "Did you finally get some sleep?"

J. T. nodded and rubbed his eyes.

"You mentioned something about drowning."

His friend stiffened then consciously relaxed. *Odd behavior*, Mike thought. He'd never seen that before. "Bad dreams?"

"Something like that," J. T. replied. "Nothing to worry about."

"Good. Ready for some breakfast?"

"You betcha."

"Oh, by the way. What do you get when you cross an insomniac with a dyslexic agnostic?"

"A little early for this, isn't it?" J. T. asked.

"Never. That's the price of breakfast."

J. T. rested his forehead on the hatch. "OK, OK. Go for it. What do you get?"

"Someone who lies awake at night wondering if there really is a dog."

J. T. considered it with a raised eyebrow. "On a scale of one to ten, that's about a four."

Mike got to his feet, the sailboat rocking to his movement. "Everybody's a critic."

By that afternoon, they had rounded Davidson Rock to the east and turned north, tacking back and forth into the wind as they made for Thatcher Pass, west of Anacortes.

The day had turned bright with sun, and the wind brought a light white froth to the waves. The sailboat leapt and bucked as it danced across the water, its sails full and straining.

Mike kept a steady hand on the tiller, and J. T. braced his feet on the opposite side of the cockpit as the sailboat heeled over in the wind. "Now we're cooking!" Mike grinned. Spray from the bow rained over them.

"Cooking, huh?" J. T. mumbled, grimacing as he wiped the spray out of his eyes with the sleeve of his sweatshirt.

"A little too close to the edge for you?" Mike called.

"Maybe. I'm just not the sailor you are."

Mike let the bow shift slightly, backing away from the wind a bit. The sailboat eased back to a more even passage, and the sound of the wind in the rigging quieted. "That's OK. Ann won't even get in the boat."

"Really?"

"Yeah. If you can't turn the key or pull to the curb, she doesn't want any part of it. Besides, she's got some church thing going this weekend."

J. T. gave him a long look. "I thought you said she had a seminar."

Mike colored, looked away.

"What's up, roomie?"

"You might not want to know, J. T."

His friend glanced up to the telltale mounted on the top of the mast, saw which way the wind was blowing, then looked back at him. "Trouble in paradise?" J. T. asked.

Mike took a deep breath then averted his eyes. "Ann and I . . . we've been 'growing apart' over the years. Her work at the university, mine at Boeing. You know what it's like. If you want to be a success, you have to work at it. Takes time and energy and dedication. There just wasn't that much left for each other. Then one day I realized that I wasn't going to make it to the top. I could work more and more hours, score the overtime, but I wasn't skilled enough, smart enough and young enough to make it. Suddenly it didn't mean as much to me. That's when I bought the boat."

"How did Ann feel about all this?"

"She said it was just my midlife crisis, and I'd get over it. She didn't want anything to do with the boat, and she was still moving up the promotion ladder at the hospital, so she didn't understand."

J. T. nodded and remained silent. The sound of the wind and the waves quieted too. Waiting.

"I had an affair."

Mike couldn't bring himself to even look at J. T. The details didn't matter. He had been weak, he had failed Ann, and he had dishonored his wedding vows. He was guilty, and he knew it.

"Does Ann know?"

Mike shook his head. "I don't think so. Maybe. She's very smart."

"Have you talked with a professional about this?"

Mike snorted. "I have very little faith in professionals," he replied. "I know some of them. And they're as screwed up as I am. How are they going to help?"

"I don't know," J. T. shrugged. "Maybe they can't. But they may be able to suggest some things to help improve your marriage. Wouldn't that be worth some effort? What would you be willing to do to save your marriage, to have it back the way it was or better?"

Mike didn't have a ready answer, and that began to bother him more than he cared to admit. Nightfall found them anchored off a sand spit on the northeast end of Lopez Island. The wind had died completely, the water reflecting the rose and peach colors of the sunset. They were not alone. Mike counted three other sailboats and a powerboat anchored to the buoys offshore, cooking smells and the quiet sounds of conversation drifting across the water.

He and J. T. sat in the cockpit, spooning chili out of a common pot into stoneware bowls. One star at a time, the night came alive with little lights as the sun set behind the island.

"Knock, knock," J. T. said.

Mike smiled. "Who's there?"

"Orange."

"Orange who?"

"Orange you glad I came along?"

Mike nodded thoughtfully. "Actually, it's good to get it off my chest finally. Sometimes I think the Catholics have the right idea about confession."

"You and Ann are my friends," J. T. said. "If I can do anything to help, I will."

"You already have. You asked me a question that's made me think."

He had finally admitted to himself he wasn't sure whether he cared if his marriage improved or not. That admission had startled him, because it was not the way he wanted to be. He wanted to care about Ann. He wanted Ann to care about him. And the path they were walking was driving them farther and farther apart.

"I remember when I first met her. It was a Hard Times party at Laurelwood our junior year. She looked so good in grubbies I couldn't help thinking how great she'd look in a dress."

J. T. slurped a spoonful of chili. "It always seemed like you two belonged together. Even then."

Mike set the bowl of chili down untouched and covered his eyes with his hands. "What do I do now?" he asked.

"I haven't a clue," J. T. answered directly. "But maybe you do."

Easter morning. The sun rose unusually warm for an early spring day in the San Juans. After a light breakfast, they'd weighed anchor and begun motoring back through Thatcher Pass toward Anacortes, their final destination. Mike went about his duties quietly, and J. T. left him alone for the most part, until the sun was fully up.

"On Friday," he mused, "you asked me if I remembered how we used to believe we could make a difference." He paused, holding Mike's full attention. "I think we still can, though maybe not on the scale we first thought. Every day that we live as part of the lives of other people, we make a difference. Sometimes that difference isn't good; maybe it's canceled out by other things, but it's there. Everything we do or don't do affects the people around us whether we know it or not . . . whether they know it or not."

"You're saying my affair affected my marriage, even if Ann doesn't know about it."

"Yes, but even before that, you affected the marriage. You'd lost confidence in yourself, you found yourself unable to continue the corporate rat race. You withdrew from it to this boat, where Ann wouldn't follow. That had to have some result."

"I didn't do this all by myself, you know."

"Granted," J. T. replied. "Just as you have an effect on Ann, she has an effect on you. But you are the only person you can control or change. It's up to you to make a difference."

J. T. jumped from the gunwale of the sailboat to the dock, caught the line Mike tossed, and secured it to the cleats. Mike was faintly surprised at the difference he'd noticed in his friend since he'd wobbled on board two days ago. He tossed J. T.'s duffel bag to him, locked up the cabin, and joined his friend on the dock. "Mike, I'm sorry if I overstepped my bounds here."

He put a hand on J. T.'s shoulder. "You're my friend, J. T. Friends go 'where angels fear to tread.' I'm glad you did. I was trying to pretend it would all go away. Unfortunately, it *is* all going away. If I don't do something, my marriage is over."

"Do you know what you're going to do?"

"No, but I know where I'm going to start. I'm going to sell the boat. I use it to get away from the problems, and that's the opposite of what I need to do."

"The boat's not the problem," J. T. said.

"True. But it's a symptom of the problem. As long as I'm here with the boat, Ann won't be with me. And that's what I want more than anything else."

"It may take some time."

Mike nodded. "I know. The trouble didn't happen overnight. It won't get solved overnight either. But I've got to start somewhere and hope that there's still time to make a difference."

J. T. turned to face him, the sun glinting off his glasses, his smile nearly as bright.

"You already have."

9

FRIENDLY
FIRE

"So . . ." Karen asked as she checked the firmness of the tomatoes in the corner grocery, "you believe that God is leading you to your former classmates, one after another?"

"I'm not sure that's the most accurate description of what's happening," J. T. countered, following her with the grocery cart. "I mean I don't hear any 'still, small voice' telling me to go left or pick up the phone and dial."

"But you have to admit that what's been going on is more than a coincidence."

"Yes," J. T. agreed, picking out a package of pasta.

"Not that brand," Karen took it from him. "If we're going to have spaghetti, we have to get 100% semolina."

J. T. looked bewildered.

"Trust me, OK?" Karen said.

"I do," he said. "And that's what I do each morning with God. I trust Him to use me where I'm needed."

They went to the checkstand and paid for the groceries. J. T. picked up the single sack and followed Karen to the door. "In the Old Testament, God appeared all over the place. In the Gospels, Jesus Himself was here on earth. What's changed that nobody sees burning bushes anymore?" J. T. wondered.

Karen wasn't listening. She was looking intently out the front window of the grocery store. "Isn't that Janice? Your friend from Laurelwood?" she asked. "I didn't know she lived close by."

J. T. slipped up beside her. "She doesn't, Karen," he said, worry creeping into his voice. "She lives on the other side of town. Something's wrong."

The city bus blew to a stop, pushing a blast of hot air in front of it, smelling of diesel and warm rubber. Janice Whitman boarded, dropping her three quarters into the receptacle, nodding at the driver, whom she didn't recognize, and looking for an empty seat. This was not her normal bus. She'd been forced to work late, and she wasn't happy about it.

Sitting by himself, just behind the driver, was a large unkempt man, his matted beard and hair sticking out in unpredictable disarray. A ragged pack between his booted feet, the man clutched a gnarled, but stout, walking stick in one grimy hand. He glanced up as Janice turned to walk down the aisle, and she had a sudden fear that he would offer her the seat next to him. But his eyes didn't seem to focus on her, and he looked away again, muttering to himself. She picked an empty seat behind an older man in coveralls, reading the afternoon paper. She settled into her seat by the bus window and tried, without looking as if she was trying, to read the newspaper in the hands of the man in front of her.

Two American fighter jets had accidentally shot down two of their own helicopters on a diplomatic mission in northern Iraq. Twenty-three dead, including a United States Senator and his aides. The words ware cold and hard, and the grainy images of the wreckage strewn across the Iraqi hills stood out starkly on the paper's front page.

All those people! She gasped inwardly. *Shot down by their own side! The poor people,* her mind strayed down a forbidden path, *all hurt . . . all violated . . . by their own . . ."* she almost said *"families."* But she slammed a mental door hard against those stray thoughts, angry at herself for having weakened. Then a voice brought her back with a start.

"What're you looking at?"

Janice glanced up, locking eyes with the scraggly man she had passed coming on board. She noticed he was missing several teeth in the front of his mouth.

"What're you looking at?" he demanded again.

"I'm sorry . . . what?" she stammered, embarrassed at having been caught reading over someone's shoulder. "I was just . . ."

"I know what 'cha were doing," the man snarled. "Looking at me, weren't 'cha? Huh?"

"No," she objected, "I was just reading over this man's shoulder!" She started to babble about knowing that wasn't exactly courteous, and how it might have looked like she was staring, but she really wasn't and . . . but the disheveled passenger cut her off in midexplanation, sliding toward her along the bus seat.

"Yeah, sure! I know! Lookin' at me!" he stomped the bus floor with his walking stick. "Lookin' at me!"

Her heart began trip-hammering, her vision darkening around

the edges, and suddenly she was ice cold. Without thinking, she yanked on the pull cord, and the bus began to slow and pull to the curb. She had only one thought: get out of there, away from that man who was coming closer, a wild leer on his face.

She only barely heard the man, whose paper she'd been reading surreptitiously, block the other man's advance by simply raising a hand and saying in a cool, clear voice, "Back off, fella. You're scaring the lady."

The side door of the bus whooshed open, and Janice was down the steps and out onto the sidewalk, the door closing behind her, the bus pulling back into traffic as she stumbled away. She turned back once as the bus disappeared, checking to make sure the scraggly man had stayed on board. He had. She put her hand to the wall of a building and tried to catch her breath.

When she looked around, she realized that she had gotten off far short of her stop.

She'd used her last little bit of change to board the bus, and she couldn't see a pay phone anywhere, not that there was anyone at home to answer. Not anymore. Now she'd have to walk the rest of the way home. She had no idea how far it was; she'd never been good at estimating distances, though she could just look at someone and tell her size after all this time at the dress shop. It was hot. She was tired and she wore heels, which were fine in the shop but were never intended for walking any distance on pavement.

She walked a couple of blocks before the pain grew to the point she couldn't ignore it any longer. Janice slipped the shoes off and, holding them in one hand, she continued on down the street in her nylons. *One more pair of pantyhose for the trash*, she conceded with a frown.

Keeping an eye on the pavement for obstacles like broken glass, she caught a glimpse of the shoes in her right hand, and her mind went wandering. Her mother had worn shoes like these because

Daddy liked them. When Daddy wasn't home, the shoes sat under her parents' bed out of the way. They weren't very practical around the house. But as soon as Daddy's car pulled into the driveway, her mother hurriedly brushed her hair, touched up her lipstick, and slipped into those shoes. Daddy wanted her to look nice when he came home from work. He wanted dinner ready, the house clean, and everything in place. Janice remembered the few times when her mother had failed.

Daddy's loud voice filled the house on those occasions, angry and painful. Janice always ran and hid when she heard that voice. One of her earliest memories was hiding under her bed as a little girl, hearing things crash in the kitchen and watching her daddy's feet pace angrily back and forth in the hall. She didn't dare close her bedroom door. Daddy didn't like it. And sometimes, when he didn't like what she'd done, he'd . . .

Janice realized with a start that she'd come to a complete stop on the hot sidewalk.

People flowed around her, and she still had a long way to go. Her vision blurred, and she found she was crying, and she couldn't stop. No one stopped to ask if she was all right. It was as if she were invisible. She raised a hand unconsciously to her cheek, touching the place where Daddy had hit her back then. As she had gotten older, there had been lots of reasons for him to do that. She just couldn't seem to do anything right.

Suddenly her breath caught short, her heart began to race. Janice, locked in her memories, relived the night Daddy had come into her room with beer on his breath. He had leaned over, and when she pretended to be asleep, he had shaken her.

"You're getting to be a big girl," he'd said, the words slurred from the alcohol. "But you'll always be Daddy's little girl, won't you?" The last words had carried menace in them.

"Yes, Daddy," she'd whispered.

He'd touched her then, his big work-hardened hand hot and clammy even through the nightgown Janice had worn.

"Yes, Daddy," she repeated. "Please, Daddy. Don't hurt me, Daddy."

The words had become a mantra. She'd said them so she wouldn't hear him breathing, until she couldn't feel his hands or smell the sick, sweet beer or, finally, anything else.

"Hey, lady. You OK?"

Janice ran. She ran without looking at the pavement or noticing when she came to crosswalks. Tears blinded her, and her breath came in ragged sobs. Daddy had hurt her, and he'd kept on hurting her. So she ran. It was the only thing she knew to do. Run. Blindly. As fast and as far as she could.

Except that she had run from Daddy to someone just like him.

The fire in her lungs finally slowed her run to a walk. Her face was wet with tears, and now that she had opened the door to the memories and the feelings, she couldn't close them off again. They rose up like a tidal wave, crashed over her, and swept her away.

Mother never left him. Despite the beatings. But Janice had finally escaped, the only way she could, the only way Daddy would allow. She got married. And for a little while she lived warm in the belief that her husband loved her so much he would never raise his hand against her in anger.

She was wrong.

At first he just tried to control her, refusing to allow her to work, stopping her from volunteering at church functions, telling her what she should wear, what she should fix for dinner, and what she needed to do each day. When he finally hit her because she'd disagreed with him about how he spent the household money, she almost expected it. But she was not like her mother. After he apologized, after they ate a silent dinner, after they had gone to bed, she dressed quietly, packed a few things, and left.

The divorce was quick and brutal. She lost everything except her personal belongings, and the emotional cost was even higher. People at the church told her to forgive him and turn the other cheek. She refused. Her father disowned her, told her she was unwelcome in his home, though that was more a relief than a threat. The one person she felt might understand—her mother—remained completely silent. When her father died a year later of a heart attack, she didn't even go to the funeral.

"Jan?"

The voice that called her name brought her up out of the flood of memory. She drew a deep breath and couldn't remember where she was.

"Jan, are you OK?"

It was J. T., a friend from long ago. He and a woman that must be his wife had just come out of a little neighborhood grocery store. He was holding a paper bag with a package of celery sticking out of the top.

"J. T.! What a . . . a . . . surprise!"

She stood there, her face streaked with tears, her hair falling around her face, her shoes in her hand, standing in her stocking feet, trying to smile and pretend. And then she just gave it up and began to cry.

The woman took her gently by the shoulders, guided her over to a little bench, and eased her down. J. T. set the groceries down beside the bench. He sat down next to her, took a handkerchief from his pocket, and held it out. She couldn't seem to stop sobbing.

Finally, the woman just put her arms around her and held her close. Let her cry. Said the things a parent is supposed to say to a child who's skinned her knee. The comforting things. The soft whispered nothings that mean everything. Her father had never done that.

Her mother couldn't. But this woman Janice didn't even know—who said her name was Karen—took her in her arms and let her be a little girl again.

It took some time, but she explained what had happened. Everything. She had never had anyone to confide in before. J. T. and Karen just listened, asking an occasional question. When she finished, J. T. sighed and sat back on the bench.

"This was going on when you were at the academy?" he asked.

Janice nodded. "That's one of the reasons I rarely went home, even on holidays. I usually went with friends."

"I never even suspected."

"I got very good at hiding the bruises."

"But you always seemed so happy to me."

"I was. The academy was the only place I could go where I was safe."

J. T. shook his head in disbelief.

"How many other people at school were like you?" he wondered. "How many that we knew nothing about."

Karen stood suddenly.

"We live just across the street in that apartment complex," she pointed out. "Why don't you come home with us for dinner? We can drive you home afterward."

"You bet. We'd be happy to have you," J. T. said. "We're having spaghetti. You like garlic bread?"

Janice nodded, looking up at Karen.

"That's my specialty," he explained, "because it's hard to screw it up."

Janice giggled and covered her mouth with her hand. It felt good, that laughter. She could get used to it.

10

FOR
LOVE'S SAKE ONLY

Karen spotted the wedding invitation almost immediately among the clutter of mail on the kitchen table. "Is this what I think it is?" she asked but didn't wait for an answer. Carefully she broke the seal on the outer envelope.

J. T. hung his coat in the closet then just stood leaning against the wall, watching his wife smile as she read the invitation.

"It's Kasey! She's getting married! Our little girl is getting married!"

"Well, we knew that," J. T. protested mildly. "We just didn't know when."

"You know what I mean. I've got to call Trish, let her know we're coming."

"I'm sure Brian James and Trish never doubted that we'd be there for our goddaughter's wedding. What I want to know is are they sure she's old enough?"

Karen turned toward him, her eyes watery with emotion. "That's just the sort of thing a father should say," her voice caught. "We'd have made good parents, wouldn't we?"

J. T. took her in his arms. "You bet. Now call Trish and tell her we're coming. And I want to talk to Brian James before you hang up."

———————————

He felt sick to his stomach. It was just a bad case of nerves; he was pretty sure.

He flushed the toilet, washed his hands carefully, then rinsed his mouth out trying to take the taste away. It wasn't anything he'd eaten for breakfast. He hadn't been able to eat anything for breakfast, so it had to be dinner last night that he'd just thrown up.

"Brian? You OK?"

"Yeah, honey. I'm fine. Just a rampaging case of nerves." He opened the bathroom door into the pastor's office. Trish was waiting for him. She looked wonderful all dressed up. "You clean up real good," he smiled.

Trish whacked him on the arm. "You'd think you were the one getting married, all this 'nerves' bit," she teased. "I don't remember you being this nervous on our wedding day."

"I wasn't," he admitted, hugging her. "I knew absolutely that marrying you was the best thing that would ever happen to me."

Trish risked her makeup and kissed him. Then she scrubbed the lipstick off his mouth with a tissue. "So . . . what's got you spooked?" she asked.

"This is our Kasey we're talking about," Brian explained. "The little girl who started to learn to play the flute, the guitar, the clarinet, and then decided they weren't for her after we'd bought the instruments."

"She's hardly a little girl anymore, Bri." Trish patted his cheek.

"That's another thing that's been on my mind. She may not be a little girl anymore, and she's not a grownup yet either."

"She's twenty-three, dear. That's old enough to know her own mind. And as for not being a 'grownup,' well, don't hold that against her. You haven't quite been exemplary in that department either," she grinned shamelessly.

"OK, OK, but what about Mark?"

"What about Mark? He's a fine young man!"

" 'Young' is the operative word here. He's what? Twenty-one? How's Kasey supposed to look up to a husband younger than she is?"

Trish shook her head. "You really are a piece of work, you know that? She's not supposed to look up to him. He's not supposed to look up to her. They're supposed to work together and look ahead. To go wherever God leads them. I'd forgotten how 'stone age' you could get when you're nervous."

"But you love me?"

She smiled widely. "I love you," she agreed. "More than anything."

The door to the pastor's study swung open and Gary popped his head in. "Hey, Dad, you through throwing up yet?"

"For the time being," he said. "Why aren't you doing something constructive, like decorating the get-away car?"

"All taken care of," Gary answered. "Some of my best work."

"So why are you harassing your mother and me?"

"Part of my job. It's in the contract I signed when I joined this outfit. Besides, you said you wanted to know when Uncle Jon and Aunt Karen showed up."

"They're here?"

"No. Just yanking your chain. Of course they're here. They're waiting for you in the foyer."

Uncle Jon and Aunt Karen weren't really related to them at all.

They were the kids' godparents. He and Trish had graduated from Laurelwood Academy with Jon. Jon had been his best man at their wedding a month later. A few years later, after the kids had come along, Brian had learned that Jon and Karen couldn't have children of their own.

He and Trish got together and asked the two of them to be the kids' godparents. Karen had cried. And even Jon Thomas—Brian always used his friend's full first and middle name while everybody else called him "J. T."—had gotten a little misty himself.

Some days he envied Jon Thomas and Karen for having a life free of children.

Other days he felt sorry for them.

On days like today . . . he didn't know how he felt.

"Jon Thomas!" he called across the foyer of the church. "Karen!"

His friends turned at the sound of his voice, smiling even before they saw him and Trish. "Brian James!" J. T. called back, matching the ritual with his own first and middle names. "And the long-suffering Trish!"

Brian caught J. T.'s hand in his own and was glad of the strength he felt there. Karen and Trish hugged each other like long-lost sisters. Gary hovered on the outskirts while the greetings took place.

"Gary," J. T. loudly whispered, "has he thrown up yet?"

"All morning long," the boy answered. "Nobody can use the bathroom."

Everyone laughed.

"You always did that just before midterms and finals," J. T. reminded him. "And the day of graduation, I thought we were going to have to give you a paper bag, just so you could march down the aisle."

"Some things never change," Trish smiled. "Like good friends. I'm so glad you both could make it."

"Wouldn't miss this for the world," Karen replied. "She's like our own daughter, too, thanks to you two." She dabbed at her eye with a tissue from her purse.

Trish took Karen by the arm, and they went off to the bathroom to check their makeup, leaving Brian and J. T. alone. Gary had wandered off somewhere. That gave Brian the chance to ask his friend a favor.

"Jon Thomas, I have a request."

"How can I help?"

"At the reception, would you give a toast for Kasey and Mark? I would do it, but I'll be honest—I don't trust my voice under the circumstances."

"Don't worry, Brian." J. T. put his hand on Brian's shoulder. "I'd be honored."

Brian tried to thank him, but his voice caught, and he ended up just smiling crookedly and shrugging.

"You're not handling all this real well, are you?" J. T. asked.

"I don't know. They seem so young!" he finally got out.

"You and Trish were even younger," J. T. reminded him.

"And we had our problems because of it. Especially when Kasey was born less than a year later. We were still kids, and the world was a lot more forgiving than it is now."

"Brian James," J. T. corrected him, "you and Trish survived, not because the world was easier but because you both loved each other so much. You must have faith."

"Faith?"

"Yes. That you raised Kasey right, that she and Mark love each other just as you and Trish did, and that God will watch over them like He's watched over all of us. You've been blessed, Brian!" J. T. punched him on the shoulder. "Be happy about it!"

Brian grinned sheepishly.

"You know . . . something that might help . . . have Trish's folks showed up yet?"

Brian nodded.

"You might spend a couple of minutes with her dad. Ask him how he felt when you and Trish got married. You might be surprised how similar your experiences are."

"I don't know, Jon Thomas," Brian wavered. "That might not be such a good idea. He wasn't in favor of the marriage. In fact, though you probably didn't know it, he almost refused to come to the ceremony."

"*Hmmm.* No. I didn't know that. Well, it was just a thought." J. T. glanced over Brian's shoulder. "Here comes Karen. I know that you and Trish have stuff to do, so we'll leave you to it and go find our seats."

"We're glad you're here, Jon Thomas."

"So am I, Brian. See you afterward."

Trish's dad hadn't liked the idea of his daughter getting married right out of high school. He'd wanted her to go on to college and "make something out of her life." And when she'd told him she was pregnant with Kasey, he just about hit the roof. Her mother had been much more understanding, and she'd been the one who helped Trish get ready for the baby. Her father wasn't sure that Brian would amount to anything, that he was even worthy of his daughter. Brian liked Trish's mother well enough, but even now, his relationship with her father was strained.

"Kasey wants to see you, Bri," Trish whispered in his ear. She seemed a little tense.

"Something wrong?"

"I'm not sure," she admitted. "Maybe just the jitters. She comes by that rightly enough. But she asked for you."

He felt suddenly warm. His little girl, even though she was going away, still needed him. "I'll take care of it. How long till the service?"

"About half an hour. But don't worry about time. Do what needs doing. I'll handle things out here."

Brian touched his wife's cheek with his fingertips. "I can always count on you."

"Always," Trish smiled back at him.

He knocked on the door to the room that had become the dressing room for all the women in the wedding party. Kasey's best friend answered the door and ushered him in, then she and the other two girls left in a rustle of perfumed lace. Only Kasey remained, seated in a wash of white satin and crinoline.

She was beautiful!

"You look so much like your mother on her wedding day," Brian said proudly.

Kasey began to cry. He strode across the room, fished a clean handkerchief out of his pocket, and set about comforting his daughter. He hoped he seemed calm and collected on the outside, but he was in turmoil within.

"What's the matter, Boo Boo?"

It was her little girl nickname, partly because she loved watching old Yogi the Bear cartoons and partly because when she skinned her knees or elbows, he'd always been the one she came to for first aid, for cleaning up the "boo boos."

"It's never going to be the same, is it, Daddy?"

Brian sat up. His daughter had just voiced his very own fear. He floundered for a second. "I'm not sure what you mean. Things will change. You're becoming a wife and someday maybe a mother. But you'll always be my daughter."

"But it will never be like it was."

"No, Boo Boo. You're right. But then, it's never been 'like it was.'" Kasey dabbed at her eyes with the handkerchief, trying not to smear her makeup. Brian could see it wasn't going to work, but that was the least of the problems at the moment. "Right now, it's not like it was when you were a baby or when you started school or when you had your first date. This is just one more part of growing up."

"But what if I made the wrong choice?" she asked.

"About Mark? About getting married?"

Kasey nodded.

"Sometimes that happens too. Adults don't always make the right choices. But if it's any help, I've watched you make decisions as you've grown up, and you do pretty well. I have faith in you, that you've made the right choice here. Mark is a good young man, with good parents."

Brian took his daughter's hand in his own and held on tight. "That doesn't mean you won't have problems. Your mother and I had our share. We were younger than you two, you know."

"What if I don't have what it takes? What if I can't make it work?"

He bent forward and kissed her on the cheek. "That's why God gave us families. To back each other up. You haven't stopped being a part of this family, and Mark hasn't stopped being part of his. He's joined ours, and you've joined his. We're all stronger because of it. You may not see it now. There are so many questions in the way. But eventually, you may find yourself explaining this to your own daughter at her wedding someday. Or Mark will," he added.

Kasey leaned forward and hugged him. She was his little girl then, but when she straightened and stood up, she was a young woman on her wedding day. He left her and her friends behind to do "reconstruction" on Kasey's makeup, and he rejoined Trish in the foyer greeting guests.

"How is she?" Trish asked in a whisper.

"A little scared, but she's getting over it."

"I knew you'd get it fixed. She loves to listen to you."

Brian sighed.

"What was that for?"

"I was just thinking," he said with a shrug, "how nice it would be if your father came up to me and said he'd changed his mind. That after all these years, he'd decided he was wrong and that you'd made the right choice marrying me."

Trish turned away from all the commotion and looked him square in the eye. "I did make the right choice marrying you," she said, the force of her will apparent. "Daydreams are nice, and I don't want to rain on your parade, but if you think my father will ever admit he was wrong about anything, then you have a better chance playing the lotto. He's not going to do it. Even if he's changed his mind, he'll never admit it."

Brian nodded and dropped his eyes. Trish touched his face with both her hands.

"What he never understood was that I did exactly what I wanted to do with my life. No regrets."

"None?"

"Well, almost none," she smirked and pinched his cheeks.

Brian looked up over his wife's shoulder and saw their daughter sweep out of the dressing room with her three friends in her wake.

"Don't look now," he whispered, "but here comes the bride," and he kissed Trish on the mouth, laughing for the sheer joy of it.

The ceremony went as ceremonies do, *almost* the way practice had went. The little flower girl walked gravely down the aisle tossing handfuls of rose petals about her as she went. Then, just as gravely, she began to pick them all up again, just as she had done during practice. When Kasey and Mark went to light the central marriage candle, an errant breeze blew it out, and they had to go back and light it again while an usher found the open door and closed it.

The words were said, the promises made, the blessings spoken, and it was over.

The reception was loud and joyful, full of dressed-up people, presents wrapped in pastels, and music in the background. During a quiet moment, Gary tapped his father on the shoulder.

"Dad, Mom, I'd like you to meet Paige."

The young lady with a generous smile had copper-colored hair down her back and clear white skin. She was terrified. That kind of thing always brought out the best in Brian.

"Good to meet you, Paige," he said, echoed quickly by Trish.

The two young people had met in a class at college. She was studying chemical engineering and though Gary was a communications major, they had had a general class together. They had been dating ever since.

"Our children seem to make good choices," Trish whispered in his ear after Paige and Gary had gone off together.

Brian nodded, his heart too full to trust his voice. At that moment, he heard the gentle clinking sound of a spoon on the side of a crystal goblet. Abruptly the noise level at the reception dropped. Jon Thomas stood near Kasey and Mark, a glass of sparkling cider in his hand.

"One of the benefits of a liberal arts education," he said with a grin, "is that you always have an appropriate quote for the occasion. This one is by Elizabeth Barrett Browning:

If thou must love me, let it be for naught except for love's sake only. Do not say I love him for his smile—his look—his way of speaking gently—for a trick of thought that falls in well with mine, and certain brought a sense of pleasant ease on such a day—for these things in themselves, Beloved, may be changed, or change for thee—and love, so wrought may be unwrought so. Neither love me for thine own dear pity's wiping my cheeks dry—a creature might forget to weep, who bore thy comfort long, and lose thy love thereby. But love me for love's sake, that evermore thou mayst love on, through love's eternity.

"We wish you life and love and laughter," J. T. appended, "and 'happy ever after.'" He raised the goblet, and everyone drank.

Later in a quiet moment, when everyone had forgotten Brian and Trish, they stood together watching everything. "Trish?"

"Um-hmm?" she asked, her voice dreamy and soft beside him as she leaned on his arm.

"Did things turn out the way you figured they would?"

Trish looked up at him, and Brian could see tears in her eyes. "No," she said in a throaty whisper, "better." And she hugged him so hard he hoped she'd never let go.

11

CASTING
BREAD

J. T. handed his wife the invitation, carefully inked on the good stationery. She read it quickly, proofreading. "You think anybody'll come?" he asked.

Dear Laurelwood Alumni,
      Twenty-five years is a long time. For some of us, it's been a very hard time. It might be worthwhile to get together again, to share our successes and our failures with the people who meant so much to us as we were growing up. There is a beach near Garibaldi on the Oregon coast where some of us found out how precious life can be, how fragile. We'd like you to join us there.

"I don't know," Karen answered. "It's always tough to get away on a moment's notice." Then she smiled and handed the invitation back to him. "But let's try anyway," she said.

"Tell me how it all began," Ken said.

"You already know that," J. T. replied. "You were there too."

The dog strained at the leash in J. T.'s hand. There was so much to smell here on the beach, hidden in the sharp-edged grass growing out of the sand and bending in the stiff breeze. Karen walked beside him, her hand on his arm.

"I'm not talking about that. That's ancient history." Ken brushed it aside with a wave of his hand. "Something's happening now, and you're at the center of it. A story."

J. T. shook his head. "You're not even close, Ken."

Ken refused to believe it. "Look, J. T. I've talked to a lot of the others here in the last couple days. Every single one of them has a story to tell, and they have two things in common."

J. T. stopped and turned his attention fully on the man walking with him. Ken was more of an acquaintance than a friend, but he'd been there twenty-four years ago. On the very same beach outside the little Oregon coastal town of Garibaldi. He'd been one of the links, one of the hands who'd reached out through the surf and helped bring them all back to the shore. Ken had even written a story about it and gotten it published.

"What do they have in common?" Karen asked, her hand tightening on J. T.'s arm.

Ken raised two fingers. "The first one is, we were all here that day when people needed help. And the second one is you, J. T."

"Me?"

Ken nodded. "All of them say you suddenly turned up in their lives again, some for the first time since graduation. Some say you were always there but that you'd gotten more intense suddenly."

"It's been on my mind lately," J. T. admitted. "What happened here. It seemed important to make contact again. We used to mean so much to each other. I wanted to know what had happened to everybody."

"There's more to it than that."

"Why do you say that?" Karen asked.

Ken shook his head. "I trust my instincts. There's a story here; I can smell it."

"Why do you want to know this 'story' so badly?" J. T. wondered.

"I tell stories," Ken smiled. "That's what I do . . . who I am. Wherever people gather around campfires, there have been people like me, carrying on the history of the tribe, the traditions. Making sure that everybody knows where they come from, so they can know where they're going."

J. T. agreed. "That's important, all right."

"So . . . you going to tell me, or what?"

J. T. grinned widely, sunlight flashing off his glasses. " 'Or what,' I think," was all he said. Then he let the dog drag him and Karen forward, following her nose on to the beach. Ken stood with his hands on his hips, frustrated, watching them go. He didn't follow them, but he looked like that's what he wanted to do.

"That wasn't very nice," Karen said with a nudge.

"He's resilient. He's not through yet."

"Are you going to tell him about the dream? About the angel?"

J. T. shook his head. "The angel's not the point. But as soon as I mention what happened, that's what he'll fix on."

"You think he won't believe you?" Karen asked.

"That's not even important. But it would draw his attention away from what is important. I won't do it."

"How about the others?"

J. T. smiled. "That's not why they're here."

On the margin between the surf and the dry sand, J. T. and Karen found Dave Turner and his wife, Nancy, on their knees sculpting sand into a large castle, with the help of Gene and his daughter Lindsey. Gene was busy with a spray bottle, fixing some of the sand into place as it dried. Lindsey, who was pregnant, worked with a hand trowel on the moat at Nancy's direction. Dave was attempting to form an arched gate without much luck. There was a lot of laughter and jubilant instruction shouted back and forth. They didn't even notice J. T. and Karen.

A little farther down the beach, William Kelly and Tom Jenkins played with a Frisbee, snapping the little plastic disk back and forth at each other with dedicated energy. William had quit his job at the restaurant and applied for loans and grants to go back to school. He intended to get his credentials updated and return to teaching. He was even on speaking terms with his children and his ex-wife.

Tom wasn't. He was still having difficulty sleeping, though the nightmares had pretty much ended. He was talking to a counselor now, and, he had told J. T. wryly, his refrigerator had real food in it now.

Davis Gregory had surprised everyone by showing up. He'd made no secret, the last time J. T. had spoken to him, that he'd wanted to forget what had happened on this beach all those years ago. Turned out that Davis had never learned to swim, and when everyone had rushed out into the surf to help, he'd hung back in the shallows, half-scared out of his mind. He'd judged himself a coward for all those long years. He and his son were dressed in matching sweat suits, practicing kata in the sand barefoot. His wife hadn't come.

Ann and Mike Anthony passed J. T. and Karen walking the opposite direction down the beach. They weren't holding hands or leaning against each other, but they were talking. Ann made some point more vivid with a slashing gesture. Mike shook his head and made his own comment. J. T. couldn't hear what they said, just the passion in their voices.

Near the edge of the beach, where the driftwood overlapped the grass-covered dunes, Janice Whitman had laid down a large towel away from the wind. She'd slathered on sunblock, put on a big sun hat and sunglasses, and was reading. She glanced up and waved at J. T. and Karen as they strolled by then went back to her book.

Brian and Trish had brought their son Gary and his girlfriend, Paige, with them for the day. They were busy getting two brightly colored kites into the air. Brian and Trish launched theirs just as J. T. and Karen ambled by. The kite took to the wind and soared upward. Gary and Paige were a little less organized about the whole process, but it would only be a matter of time before they were successful too. Brian's laughter was swept up by the wind.

Among the missing were Alan and Marie MacRory and their girls. They couldn't afford to make the trip to join them at the beach, but they'd written to thank them for the invitation and to let them know that they were thinking of them.

"They're all here because of you," Karen said.

J. T. shook his head. "They're all here because they felt the need to make contact. Because we all meant something to each other a long time ago, and we wonder if that 'meaning' is still there."

"Is it?"

"Oh yes." He smiled. "It is. We were brought together in a single moment of time to help each other. We may have gone our separate ways, but the reason for our existence has never changed. We're here to help each other. And by doing that, we are enriching and sustaining ourselves."

Then J. T. kicked off his shoes, stripped off his socks, and rolled up his pant legs. "Wanna go wading?" he asked with a grin.

"That water's cold!" Karen protested.

"Invigorating!"

"Freezing!"

"OK, it's cold. You wanna go?"

"Sure!" Karen grinned back. "But no body-surfing."

"Not a chance," J. T. replied. "I may be a slow learner, but I'm not stupid."

Hand-in-hand they skipped down to the surf's edge, jumping back and forth, playing tag with the waves. The dog busied herself barking at them.

It had begun with light in the darkness . . . and a man going nowhere special . . . and a dream that didn't end when the sun came up. And that has made all the difference.

IF YOU ENJOYED THIS BOOK . . .

you might enjoy reading other books
in our Sycamore Tree line.

Prayer Warriors
Guardians
Eleventh Hour
Midnight Hour
Be My Angel
It's Time to Stop Rehearsing What We Believe
The Journal of a Not-So-Perfect Daughter

Turn the page to find out more.

PRAYER WARRIORS

Céleste perrino Walker

Open your eyes to the struggles going on in the lives of seemingly ordinary people dealing with painful realities. Raise the curtain on the battle behind the scenes, where angels and demons fight for the eternal destiny of each human. In every case, angels stand ready to protect the children of God.

But in this tightly woven story of embattled believers, it is not the might of God's angels that turns the tide against the plans of the demons. That power comes when the hands of a warrior are folded in prayer.

ISBN: 0-8163-1359-8. US$12.99, Can$18.99.

GUARDIANS

Céleste perrino Walker

Guardians brings the power of prayer to life. Picking up where she left off in the bestselling *Prayer Warriors*, Céleste perrino Walker continues to weave the remarkable story of ordinary people struggling with life and with their relationships with God. Prayer—their own and the prayers of those who "stand in the gap" for them—is their only hope as spiritual warfare wages all around them. Behind the scenes, angels and demons fight to influence their minds and direct their decisions.

Guardians makes fascinating reading. But more than that, it may change you, the way you see the world, and the way you pray.

ISBN: 0-8163-1407-1. US$12.99, Can$18.99.

ELEVENTH HOUR

Céleste perrino Walker and Eric Stoffle

A religious coalition with a strong political agenda. A movement for all churches to "get together." Believers doubting whether or not holding onto a few "different" beliefs is worth being ridiculed by the world—especially by other Christians. Strange, incurable plagues.

A new end-time story? Or headlines from today's newspapers? *Eleventh Hour* is the story of a father searching for his lost daughter, a doctor searching for a cure. It is the story of a man who believes he is working for God in a political movement. It is the story of an FBI agent working deep undercover and his sister's struggle with addiction—and with the challenge of accepting the truth.

ISBN: 0-8163-1649-X. US$12.99, Can$18.99.

MIDNIGHT HOUR

Céleste perrino Walker and Eric Stoffle

The exciting sequel to *Eleventh Hour*. With time winding down, the world hurtles toward certain destruction. But whle the wicked seek to blame and destroy the Remnant for their misery, God's faithful discover peace, hope, and courage. Whose side will you be on just minutes to Midnight?

ISBN: 0-8163-1698-8. US$12.99, Can$18.99.

BE MY ANGEL

Harriet Canne

Things don't always appear what they seem. This is what Merideth discovers as she searches for answers about life, death, and what comes afterwards. It isn't until a terrifying encounter with a ouija board that she realizes she's been lured into the dark world of the occult by a rather innocent-looking deck of cards—angel cards. A story of the search for truth and the subtle deceptions of Satan.

ISBN: 0-8163-1708-9. US$11.99, Can$17.49

IT'S TIME TO STOP REHEARSING WHAT WE BELIEVE AND START LOOKING AT WHAT DIFFERENCE IT MAKES

Reinder Bruinsma

Finally, a book that answers the question "What difference does it make?" Even if you've grown up in the church and taken all the religion classes, sometimes there seems to be more questions than answers. Does what we believe really matter in the way we live? Does being an Adventist go beyond being in church on Saturday monring?

With stories and illustrations that bring the book to life, Reinder Bruinsma, a long-time church pastor and administrator, honestly and clearly explores the purpose and value of each of our doctrines.

ISBN: 0-8163-1401-2. US$9.99, Can$14.49.

JOURNAL OF A NOT-SO-PERFECT DAUGHTER

Nancy Carver Abbott

This may be one of the most unique and compelling books you'll ever read.

In the pages of her journal, Nancy reaches across time to recapture her father's childhood—and her own. Growing up in the church didn't prepare her for everything life would throw at her. Through tears and laughter, she tries to understand her father's faith in God and in church. In a most open and honest way, she tries to deal with his aging, her questions, and her own feelings about God.

Nancy's journal opens her heart and her life in ways that will profoundly move you.

ISBN: 0-8163-1650-3. US$10.99, Can$15.99.